PLAYERS IN A DEADLY GAME

A man shooting for murderously high stakes with dangerously loaded dice . . .

A beautiful woman with blood on her hands and death at her heels . . .

An escaped convict clawing his way through a swamp of horror . . .

A husband betting his life on the wits of his wife . . .

A wife desperately trying to tell a doubting world that her husband is out to slay her . . .

These are just some of the unforgettable characters Alfred Hitchcock has unleashed to play nasty tricks on your nerves far, far into the night—

KILLERS AT LARGE

Killers at Large

ALFRED HITCHCOCK, EDITOR

A DELL BOOK

Published by
Dell Publishing Co., Inc.
1 Dag Hammarskjold Plaza
New York, New York 10017

ISBN: 0-440-14443-4

Printed in the United States of America
First printing—August 1978

ACKNOWLEDGMENTS

SYSTEM PLAYER by Richard Deming—Copyright © 1964 by H.S.D. Publications, Inc. Reprinted by permission of the author and the author's agents, Scott Meredith Literary Agency, Inc.

LOADED GUNS ARE DANGEROUS by Richard O. Lewis —Copyright © 1965 by H.S.D. Publications, Inc. Reprinted by permission of the author and the author's agents, Scott Meredith Literary Agency, Inc.

WELCOME STRANGER by Elijah Ellis—Copyright © 1965 by H.S.D. Publications, Inc. Reprinted by permission of the author and the author's agents, Scott Meredith Literary Agency, Inc.

COME RIDE WITH ME by Donald Honig—Copyright © 1975 by H.S.D. Publications, Inc. Reprinted by permission of the author and the author's agents, Raines and Raines.

SHERIFF PEAVY'S COSA NOSTRA CAPER by Richard Hardwick—Copyright © 1964 by H.S.D. Publications, Inc. Reprinted by permission of the Estate of Richard Hardwick and the agents for the Estate, Scott Meredith Literary Agency, Inc.

YELLOWBELLY by William Brittain—Copyright © 1975 by H.S.D. Publications, Inc. Reprinted by permission of the author and the author's agents, Scott Meredith Literary Agency, Inc.

BECAUSE OF EVERYTHING by Glenn Canary—Copyright © 1962 by H.S.D. Publications, Inc. Reprinted by permission of the author and the author's agents, Scott Meredith Literary Agency, Inc.

REFUGE by Fletcher Flora—Copyright © 1968 by H.S.D. Publications, Inc. Reprinted by permission of the Estate

CONTENTS

INTRODUCTION

I wonder if specialization might not be getting out of hand. What brings the question to mind is a cookbook I came across recently. Its recipes were devoted entirely to the bean—the bean as soup, salad, main course, dessert, and, ultimately, leftover. When we are offered lima bean sherbet after the soybean Newburgh, perhaps specialization, at least in the culinary art, has already gone too far.

True, a variety of beans was used in the recipes— fava beans, garbanzo beans, kidney beans, the aforementioned limas and soys, and so on. I can see, nevertheless, where the trend is taking us. What we are in store for, no doubt, is a cookbook that concentrates solely on the Mexican jumping bean, with a preface by a transcendental meditationist instructing us on how to get the bean to hold still while it is being slathered with a wine-and-cream sauce.

Specialization is already rampant in the medical profession. There are doctors who limit their practice to the treatment of tennis elbow and skier's frostbite, and there is an entire clinic—doctors, nurses, researchers, orderlies, etc.—that is supported by Joe Namath's knees. But even so, the possibilities for further narrowings are clearly in evidence. I can see the day when treatment of the southern section of the lower intestine will be exclusively the province of physicians from Alabama.

The trades, too, have seemingly been seized by this particular madness. Plumbers and carpenters, of course, have always had their apprentices, the young men who run and fetch. But now, I understand, the helpers are limiting themselves to specific tools. Saw apprentices run and fetch only saws, hammer apprentices run and fetch only hammers, and so forth. Construction on a new sports arena was halted for a whole day recently, I am told, when the entire corps of apprentices walked off the job in high dudgeon because an electric drill apprentice had been asked to run and fetch a finishing nail.

I learned personally how far specialization has gone in the plumbing trade not long ago. Having summoned a plumber to repair a leak, I watched, curious, as he and his assistant inspected the malfunction. Without even having opened his toolbox—or having his assistant do it—the plumber informed me that he had to return to his shop.

"This joint takes a monkey wrench," he explained to me. "I got to go back and get Joe."

"Is Joe the name of the monkey wrench," I asked, "or does someone named Joe have the monkey wrench?"

"No, I got the monkey wrench right here in my toolbox," he replied, "but Joe is my monkey wrench hander. He hands me the monkey wrench."

I indicated the assistant. "Can't this young man hand you the monkey wrench?"

"This is Frank," he informed me. "Frank is a pipe wrench hander."

I suggested that, in the absence of Joe, I perform the role of the monkey wrench hander. This caused Frank to stalk out, threatening to throw up a picket line around the house. The plumber quickly followed, advising me that he would not return, fearful that any further dealing with me might get him involved in unfair labor practices litigation.

There is no doubt in my mind that specialization will soon spread to the service field. On the airlines there will be a stewardess to serve the coffee, another to serve the tea, and a third to serve the milk. When a martini is ordered, one stewardess will bring the drink and another will come along later with the olive.

Fortunately, in the present circumstances, I can see some good in this. With overpopulation what it is, there is a need for something for all the excess people to do. If they were not specializing in some facet of some profession, trade, or service, they might all be in the business of creating suspense movies. And, although I champion the theory of competition, I have always believed that in actuality it is best suited to vocations other than my own.

In that regard, I suppose I could be accused of specializing, too, in that I have concentrated a major share of my time on producing *brilliant* suspense films. But in my defense, I would like to point out that I have never limited myself to the use of brilliance alone. I have invariably employed good taste, humor, and craftsmanship, also—not to mention luck, that blessing that seems to come to all persons of true humility.

Be that as it may, I now invite you to entertain yourself with the works of another group of specialists, the contrivers of the superb suspense tales that follow. I promise you that you will find their specialty a nerve-tingling delight.

—ALFRED HITCHCOCK

SYSTEM PLAYER

by Richard Deming

The bartender was alone when Paul Carrick entered the tavern. He had deliberately chosen six P.M. as the best time to drop in, because the hour from six to seven was normally the deadest period of the day in neighborhood taverns, and he wanted an uninterrupted period to get acquainted with the man behind the bar.

The bartender took in the touch of gray at his temples, his distinguished bearing and the expensive cut of his clothes, and said with the touch of deference Carrick invariably inspired at first sight in all bartenders, "Evening, sir."

Carrick gave him a pleasant nod and seated himself on a stool near the center of the bar. "Scotch on the rocks, please."

As the barkeep poured the drink, Carrick examined him carefully. The man was only about twenty-five, stocky and plain-featured, but with an air of good nature about him. Carrick noted he was wearing a wedding band.

"Sixty cents," the barkeep said as he set the drink on the bar.

Carrick looked pleasantly surprised. Pulling a dollar from his wallet, he said, "That's certainly reasonable. Where I come from plain bar whisky is sixty cents."

The barkeep rang up the sale and laid the change before Carrick. "Where's that?"

"Southern California."

"You're a long way from home. Just passing through town?"

"Uh-huh. I'm over at the Gatesworth." After a pause he added, "I hate to drink alone. Buy you a drink?"

"It's a little early," the bartender said, then shrugged. "I guess one won't hurt me."

He made himself a highball from a bottle beneath the bar which Carrick suspected contained nothing but colored water. He had as yet made only a cursory inspection of the town, but long experience enabled him to get the feel of a new town very quickly. Rydburg impressed him as the sort of community where such minor cheating was routinely practiced on tourists.

The bartender rang up the other forty cents left from the dollar bill.

During the next half hour Carrick bought two more drinks and simultaneously exercised his charm. No one at all came into the place, so their conversation was uninterrupted. They started with the weather, touched on baseball, then moved to the coming heavyweight championship fight. When Carrick felt they were sufficiently well acquainted, he steered the conversation in a more personal direction.

Glancing at the man's wedding band, he said, "I see you're married. At your age I'd hazard you're still honeymooning."

"Oh, we been married a couple of years."

"Any children?"

"A little girl a year old."

"Oh?" Carrick said with interest. "I have a niece that age. Got a picture of her?"

It developed that the barkeep had a wallet full of pictures, snapped at one month intervals. When Carrick made admiring noises over the collection, the young bartender smiled fatuously. Carrick knew the young man was beginning to regard him as an old friend when he poured his third drink from the bottle on the back bar instead of from the one beneath the bar.

Having established camaraderie, he asked casually, "Any action in this town?"

The barkeep raised his brows. "How you mean?"

"Poker, dice. Anything."

The young man pursed his lips. "That's illegal around here."

With a smile Carrick produced his wallet, opened it to expose the plastic-enclosed cards and laid it on the bar. "I'm not a state cop. I'm just a tourist. Check anything you want in there."

Carrick had opened the wallet so that one of the two exposed cards was a California driver's license with his photograph on it. The barkeep glanced from the photograph to his customer's aristocratically handsome face, then back to the license again.

"Paul Carrick, eh?" he said. Quickly he flipped through the other cards. "Elks, American Legion, Auto Club. You sure carry enough identification, Mr. Carrick. Mind telling me your business?"

"Investments."

"Oh." Closing the wallet and handing it back, he stuck out his hand. "I'm Joe Small."

Carrick gave the proffered hand a friendly grip. "Glad to know you, Joe."

The young man poured two more drinks and made a dismissing gesture when Carrick pushed money toward him.

"Your health," Carrick said, raising his glass. After sipping, he asked, "Well?"

"There's a joint on the edge of town," the barkeep said reluctantly. "I could give you a card to get in, but I'm not wild about doing it."

"Why? Didn't I pass muster?"

"Oh, sure. But you seem like a kind of nice guy. You know anything about Rydburg?"

"Very little. By the number of motels and hotels, I assume you have a lot of tourist business."

"We live on it," the barkeep said glumly. "It's a clip town. Even this joint. At eight o'clock the B-girls come on duty. You buy one a drink and I soak you a half a buck for colored water. And this is one of the cleaner joints. In some you flash a roll and you're likely to get Mickey Finned. At least we don't roll customers. But Glenn's Spot is about as raw as they come. If you manage to beat the crooked dice, you're likely as not to get waylaid in the alley behind the place when you walk out."

Carrick frowned. "If it's that crooked, how does it get any customers?"

"It doesn't from the locals. It's a tourist trap. And everybody doesn't get clipped. The dollar bettors get a fair enough shake. Glenn rides on house percentages so long as he doesn't get hurt. You could walk out with a couple of hundred win and nobody would give you a second glance. But get a hot streak and start shooting hundred-dollar chips, and you can bank on a dice switch. Walk out with as much as a thousand and you're just asking for a bat on the head before you reach your car."

"Don't victims complain to the police?"

The barkeep snorted. "The chief of police is Glenn's brother-in-law and the sheriff's his cousin. They're sort of silent partners, if you get what I mean."

"I understand," Carrick said, smiling. "It sounds like an interesting place."

"Well, I get a fin for every new customer I steer there. Glenn has that arrangement with most of the local bartenders. But I've got a conscience too."

"I appreciate your warning," Carrick assured him. "But I'm strictly a dollar shooter, so I could hardly get in trouble."

With a shrug the bartender opened a drawer in the back bar and took out a white business card. On its back he wrote: "Introducing Paul Carrick," and signed his name. "There's a restaurant in front, but the casino's around back," Joe Small explained. "You can't get into the casino from the restaurant. The alley door's the only way in or out. Park on the lot alongside the restaurant and walk up the alley behind the building. You'll see a shaded light over a door. Knock there and show your card. That's all there is to it."

"Thanks," Carrick said, dropping the card into his pocket and rising from his stool.

"Sure. Good luck, Mr. Carrick."

"I generally have pretty fair luck," Carrick said. "I use a system."

Joe Small grinned. "I've heard that before. The poorhouse is full of system players."

Carrick merely smiled. Offering his hand, he said, "Nice to have met you, Joe."

He left a dollar tip.

Back at the Gatesworth Hotel he found a note in his box to phone operator two at Iron Falls, Iowa. Instead of going up to his room to make the call, he got change from the desk and used the lobby phone booth.

Operator two in Iron Falls said, "One moment, please." There was about a half minute wait, then, "Here is you party, sir."

A masculine voice said, "Paul?"

"Uh-huh. Any luck?"

The man at the other end of the wire emitted a disgusted snort. "This whole section is so lawabiding, it turns my stomach. I've run into only two house games during the past week—both honest."

"There's a prospect here," Carrick said. "How soon can you get here?"

"Tomorrow easy. How's it look?"

"Perfect. The place is called Glenn's Spot, and you need a card to get in. Local bartenders keep cards on hand and do the preliminary screening. I don't imagine you'll have any trouble getting a card from a bartender."

"Check. See you tomorrow night."

"Okay. I'll hit the place about eleven P.M."

Carrick had dinner in the hotel dining room and

went to bed early. The next day he stuck to his room, going out only for meals. At ten-thirty P.M. he carried his suitcase downstairs, checked out, and paid his bill. Carrying the bag out to the hotel parking lot alongside the building, he put it in his car trunk. When he drove from the lot, he turned east.

Just beyond the city limits was a well-populated business area. A neon sign advertised GLENN'S SPOT—FINE FOODS—COCKTAILS. A parking lot alongside the restaurant was packed with cars. Carrick managed to find a vacant slot, locked the car and headed for the alley running behind the place.

On the opposite side of the alley from the casino were the rears of several business establishments, with narrow areaways between them. Except for a single shaded bulb over the door at the far end of the restaurant building, the alley was unlighted and these areaways were in dense shadow. Recalling what the young barkeep had said about big winners sometimes being waylaid in the alley, Carrick cast a mildly apprehensive glance into each areaway as he passed it.

The door beneath the shaded bulb opened immediately to his knock. A thick-featured man with a squashed nose gave him a benign smile and said, "Yes, sir?"

Carrick handed over his card.

After examining it, the doorman stepped aside and said, "Come on in."

Carrick found himself in a short, windowless hall which had another door at its far end. Closing and locking the outer door, the doorman preceded Carrick to the inner one, opened it and motioned to someone in the room beyond. The moment the door opened, a mixture of sounds rolled through it. There was the whirr of slot machines, the click of dice, the droning voices of house men calling points and winning numbers, and over it all a medley of muted conversation punctuated by an occasional feminine squeal of triumph.

The doorkeeper's broad back blocked Carrick's view of the room. After a moment's wait the doorman stepped back to allow a lean, gray-haired man of about sixty to enter the windowless hall. Closing the door into the casino behind the man, he handed him the card.

After glancing at it, the lean man extended a hand, smiled affably and said, "I'm Glenn Keyser, Mr. Carrick. You a friend of Joe's?"

Carrick shook hands and gave the casino proprietor an answering smile. "No, I just happened to wander into his bar. I don't know anyone in town."

"Tourist?"

"Uh-huh. En route from California to New York." He reached for his wallet. "I have plenty of identification."

"That won't be necessary," Keyser protested. "I'm sure Joe Small checked you out. We have to be a little careful, because this isn't exactly a legal operation. Come on in."

Courteously he held the door for Carrick to precede him. As he stepped into the room, Carrick saw that it was about thirty by fifty feet, with a bar at one end and with slot machines spaced about the other three walls. There was a roulette table, a poker table, two twenty-one games and three dice tables. There were about fifty customers in the place, only a sprinkling of them women. The women for the most part wore street clothes, though there were one or two cocktail gowns. Dress among the men varied from sport shirts and slacks to coats and ties.

"What's your lucky game?" Keyser asked.

"Dice. What's the limit here?"

"A thousand."

"On odds bets too?"

Keyser nodded. "On any bet in the house, including roulette. We rarely get a limit bet, though, except when somebody gets hot at dice and keeps doubling up." He eyed Carrick curiously.

"Just asking out of curiosity," Carrick said with a smile. "I didn't mean to give you the impression that I'm a big-time spender. My usual speed is silver dollars on the pass line."

The touch of speculative interest in the casino proprietor's eyes faded. "You'll find a lot of company here. Dollar bettors are our bread and butter." He pointed to a cashier's cage across the room. "You can buy chips over there. Good luck, Mr. Carrick."

"Thanks," Carrick said quietly.

Instead of going immediately to the cashier's cage, he moved to the bar and had a drink while he looked the place over. The dice tables were getting the best play, with from eight to ten people ringing each. In addition to the house men running the various games, he spotted one or two burly men lounging about doing nothing and tabbed them as house trouble-shooters.

Carrick waited at the bar long enough to make sure that Glenn Keyser had lost all interest in him, then walked over to the cashier's cage and drew out his wallet. He counted out ten one-hundred-dollar bills and one ten-dollar bill.

"Give me ten one-hundred-dollar chips and ten silver dollars," he said.

The cashier counted out the chips and coins and murmured a perfunctory, "Good luck, sir."

The hundred-dollar chips were bright yellow, with the figure 100 embossed in green on one side and GLENN'S SPOT embossed in the same color on the other. Carrick dropped them into the side pocket of his coat, but kept the silver dollars in his hand. He drifted over to the center dice table and found a slot directly opposite the table cashier. He stood watching the play for a time, sliding the silver dollars back and forth from one hand to the other.

In addition to himself, there were nine players ringing the table, plus the two house men. On his right was a well-dressed man of about fifty with a lovely but giggling blonde half his age. Beyond them was a middle-aged couple; both were betting from the same stack of silver dollars. At the far end of the table was a rather good-looking muscular young man of perhaps twenty-six using red five-dollar chips.

In the other direction there were four men, two having nothing before them but silver dollars, one with a sizeable stack of reds, and a plump man at the end having about two hundred dollars in ten-dollar blue chips before him.

The middle-aged woman had just fallen off when Carrick reached the table. Her husband risked a silver dollar, threw a four and took another dozen throws before he finally sevened out.

The lovely but giggling blonde was next in line. Carrick watched her make two one-dollar passes while her escort backed her up with five-dollar bets.

As she left a dollar on the pass line for the next throw, Carrick grinned at her and said, "I think you're going to fall off this time."

He laid a dollar on the no-pass line, leaned over to the lined-off section in front of the cashier and laid another in the square marked CRAPS.

The girl threw a seven.

With a rueful smile at the cashier, Carrick said, "That's the way my hunches always work out."

The man gave him a polite smile.

The blonde and her escort both doubled up, she threw a ten, then a seven. The well-dressed man passed the dice to Carrick. He bet a dollar, got eight for a point and immediately sevened off.

The dice went on down the table with no one either winning or losing any spectacular amount. The largest single bets were by the plump man at the end, who bet one way or the other on every roll, but never risked more than a single blue chip. Carrick placed a few dollar bets and had run his ten up to fourteen by the time the plump man fell off.

When the dice were passed to the muscular young

man at the opposite end of the table, he set two red chips on the pass line.

"Get on old Sam this time, folks," he announced generally. "This roll is paying for Sam's vacation. I feel seven straight passes coming on."

The middle-aged couple next to him each put a dollar on the pass line. The giggling blonde risked a dollar too, and her escort bet a red chip. Mass psychology set in and all around the table players laid their customary bets on the pass line. All except Carrick.

"Come on, mister," the young man urged. "Let's make it unanimous."

Carrick said, "I think old Sam's going to crap out," put a dollar on the no-pass line and tossed another on CRAPS.

"You'll be sor—ree," the young man said, and threw an eleven.

"I should swear off hunches," Carrick said to the cashier, and got another polite smile in answer.

"Don't pick up a dollar of your winnings, folks," the young shooter said. "Double up with old Sam and we'll break the bank. Six more passes guaranteed."

Everyone except the plump man let his bet ride. He cautiously risked only a single blue.

Carrick said, "If you can't beat 'em, join 'em," and put a silver dollar on the pass line.

"Now we're unanimous," the shooter said. "Watch old Sam make everybody rich."

He threw a seven.

"Don't touch it," he urged the group. "Five more passes are coming as sure as old Sam stands here. Let it ride."

This time even the plump man left both blue chips on the pass line. Sam threw an eight and immediately eighted back.

"I'm hotter than an Eskimo in Florida," the young man crowed as the cashier rapidly doubled stacks all around the table. "Here's how sure I am." He pushed every chip in front of him into the pass line. "Let it ride, folks. We're going all the way."

No one reached to withdraw any chips.

The stick man had not yet flicked the dice back to the shooter, waiting for the cashier to pay off the wins and for any players who wished to pick up their chips. They still lay on the table, showing the four and four which the young man had just thrown. The cashier picked them up to examine them.

It was a perfectly manipulated switch, so expert that even Paul Carrick's practiced eye might have missed it if he hadn't been watching for it. But he knew when the cashier set the dice back on the table that the original pair had been palmed.

The stick man flicked the cubes to the shooter, who scooped them up on the fly and rattled them next to his ear.

"Come on, babies," he chanted. "Seven up and stop."

Carrick timed it to the last fraction of a second. His hand came out of his coat pocket and he laid the ten yellow chips on CRAPS a split instant before the dice were cast.

The stick man had no time to grab the dice on the pretense that the roll wasn't going to reach the board and bounce, or even to call out, "No dice." Before it even registered on him that the bet had been made, he droned matter-of-factly, "Craps, six-six."

Then both he and the cashier did double takes. The cashier paused in the act of sweeping in all chips on the pass line and stared at the stack of yellow chips in disbelief.

"Craps pay eight-to-one," Carrick said with cheerful helpfulness. "Just stack eight thousand dollars next to my bet."

"Just a minute," the cashier said. "You can't make a bet after the dice were thrown."

Raising his brows, Carrick glanced around at the

other players. "Did I place my bet after the dice were thrown?"

The plump man on the end said to the cashier, "It was a legal bet. What you trying to pull?"

"Sure it was," the blonde chimed in. "I saw him place it."

The cashier flicked a nervous glance around the table and found everyone but young Sam frowning at him. The latter was still gazing disconsolately at the boxcars he had tossed.

A trifle desperately the cashier said to Carrick, "You were only betting dollars. Where'd these yellows come from?"

I bought them from the main cashier, if you want to check. They aren't counterfeit."

Glancing toward the bar, the cashier made a beckoning motion. Immediately the lean figure of the proprietor moved that way.

"Trouble, Nat?" Glenn Keyser asked pleasantly.

"This guy dropped ten yellows on craps just as the shooter threw the dice, Mr. Keyser," the cashier said. "He'd only been betting silver dollars before that."

"Are you refusing to pay the win?" Carrick demanded somewhat loudly. "What kind of a clip joint is this?"

After a mere flick of a glance at Carrick, the casino proprietor ran his gaze around the circle of players, finding expressions of awaiting hostility on all of their faces. Attracted by the dispute, other customers began to drift over from different tables to see what was going on.

"I don't get your beef, Nat," Keyser said with forced good humor. "Didn't he have the bet down in time?"

"Of course he had it down in time," the plump man on the end said testily. "If the dice hadn't come up craps, you would have scooped up his chips fast enough. What kind of stuff are you people trying to pull?"

Keyser said quietly, "Pay the man off."

"I don't have that much on the table," the cashier said sullenly.

Keyser picked up the ten yellow chips. "The main cashier will pay you off, Mr. Carrick," he said in a pleasant tone. "Come with me."

The young man named Sam said in a rueful tone. "Wiped out, down to the last penny. Guess I'll go home and hang myself." Morosely he moved in the direction of the door.

As Carrick and Keyser walked toward the cashier's cage, the casino proprietor said, "I thought you were just a dollar bettor, Mr. Carrick."

"Oh, I plunge on occasion."

"I see you do. With remarkable luck, too. Maybe this is your lucky night. We have a little private poker game in the basement where the stakes are a lot better than the open game we have up here. Like to try your luck?"

Seven house men and a marked deck, Carrick thought. He said, "No thanks. I believe I'll call it a night."

"Like one chance to double your winnings? I'll cut you cards for sixteen thousand or nothing."

Carrick merely gave his head an amused shake.

They reached the cashier's cage and Keyser laid down the ten yellow chips. "Cash these in and add eight thousand to it," he directed.

As the cashier began counting out hundred-dollar bills, Carrick watched Keyser from the corners of his eyes. When he saw the man make an almost imperceptible motion to someone across the room and simultaneously incline his head slightly toward Carrick, the latter casually glanced over his shoulder in time to catch the nod of understanding from one of the burly trouble-shooters. Carrick faced forward again, not wanting to appear interested in the burly man's actions, but certain the signal had sent him scurrying toward the door and outside.

Carrick recounted the stack of hundred-dollar bills,

found there were ninety and placed them in his inside breast pocket.

"Thanks and good-night," he said to Keyser.

"You're welcome, Mr. Carrick," the gambler said affably. "Drop in again."

The burly man Keyser had signaled was nowhere in evidence, Carrick noted, but it failed to worry him. In the short hallway between the two doors the squash-nosed doorkeeper wished him a cordial goodnight and held open the outer door for him.

There was no one in sight in the alley when the door closed behind him. Standing in the circle of light from the overhead bulb, he probed the shadows beyond.

"Over here, Paul," a voice called softly.

Approaching the areaway from which the voice came, he found the young man named Sam indolently leaning against one of the buildings which the areaway separated, playfully tossing a leather sap into the air and catching it again. A few feet beyond the young man Carrick could dimly make out the motionless figure of a man lying on the ground.

"Any trouble?" he asked.

"Naw. He walked in here blind as a bat, his eyes still adjusted to the inside light, and turned his back to me so he could watch for you to come out the door. One judo chop did it." He held out the leather sap. "See what he had planned for you?"

Carrick eyed the implement with distaste. With a chuckle the young man tossed it next to the prone figure. He and Carrick unhurriedly strolled toward the parking lot together.

LOADED GUNS
ARE DANGEROUS

By Richard O. Lewis

When George Unders answered the knock on the back door and saw the two strange men waiting there in the glow of the porch light, he guessed that this was it. It was the thing he had been more or less expecting, night after night, yet hoping would never happen.

"We'd like to use your telephone," one of them said. He was a big man with a round face and thick lips.

"It won't take us long," said the other. He was as big as his companion, but his face was more angular and was blue with a stubble of beard.

George didn't unlock the screen door. He stood with his hand hesitantly on the latch while a multitude of thoughts raced about in his head. He knew these men. Not by sight, of course. No one knew them by sight. Yet, he felt certain that these were the men he had been vaguely expecting. These were the ones who pounced out of the night onto lone coin collectors, looted them, and vanished back again into the night, leaving no witnesses. The papers had been full of their exploits for the past several months. And now they were here.

When he had first read the newspaper articles, he had taken certain precautionary measures. There was a pistol in the kitchen at his back. It was on top of the cabinet, within easy reach—provided one was standing near enough to the cabinet. It had been placed there for just such an emergency. But now that the emergency was at hand, George realized the pistol was of no earthly use to him. If these men were who he thought they were, he wouldn't dare make a try for it.

He considered slamming the wooden door and bolting it. Then he could grab the pistol and turn off the lights. Certainly they wouldn't break down the door. Or would they? Yes, they would! Now that they had let him see their faces, they would not turn back. And they were big enough to crash through the screen before he had time to bolt the door.

But what if they did merely want to use the telephone? What if their car had broken down?

There was a sudden swish of slippered footsteps at his back. Martha came up beside him. She was a round little woman with a topknot of mousey hair, pale cheeks, and eyes of pale blue. As usual, her spectacles hung halfway down over the bridge of her short nose.

"What is it, George? she wanted to know, lowering her head a trifle so she could peer over her glasses through the screen. "Who is it?"

"We'd like to use your telephone, ma'am," said the one with the round face.

"Why, of course! George, don't just stand there! Where are your manners? Let the gentlemen in."

George unlatched the screen and pushed it open. Under the circumstances, there seemed little else he could do.

Each man picked up a black valise and followed him into the lighted kitchen. George glanced at the top of the cabinet. The black butt of the pistol was plainly visible. But he couldn't make a try for it, not with the man with the round face breathing directly down the back of his neck.

Martha bustled among them, around them, and ahead of them, leading them into the living room, babbling on and on, as usual, like a meandering brook, getting nowhere in particular.

"Now you just put your things down and make yourselves comfortable," she invited. "I'll make a nice pot of tea for us all. And I believe I have some cookies."

"We don't want any tea," the round-faced one said flatly. He seated himself on the arm of a chair, his bag beside him.

"No tea?" said Martha. "Perhaps a cup of coffee, then?" She pushed her glasses up over the bridge of her nose, and they promptly fell back again to their customary resting place. She peered over them from one to the other. "Oh, goodness!" she said, suddenly, clasping her hands together in dismay. "How silly of me! Here I've gone and forgotten your names already."

"That's Mr. Blackie," said the round-faced one. "I'm Wilberforce. But you can just call me Wilber."

"Wilber," said Martha, appreciatively. "That's a real nice name! I had a cousin once—"

Poor Martha. They were poking fun at her, and she didn't even realize it. Fervently, George wished she had gone out somewhere this night. Anywhere. Anywhere so she wouldn't have to face this ordeal! But, no, Martha never went out anywhere. Starved for friendship as she was, she had made a few friends. She simply tried too hard. When callers came, she plied them with a continuous flow of food and drink, drowned them in conversation, gushed and bustled over them—and wondered why they seldom came back or invited her out.

Wilber had turned toward George. "I hear you have a large collection of coins," he said casually.

George was leaning against the open door to the stairway. He was certain now that his first guess had been right. These were the killers! He wondered how they had learned of his collection; only a few friends knew of its existence. Then, suddenly, he knew. An advertisement had appeared several months ago in a magazine offering a fabulous buy in old coins. He had answered it; he had received no reply. These men had placed the ad; they now had the name and address of every coin collector who had answered it. They had started down the list, leaving a trail of blood in their wake, and they would continue until somewhere, somehow, someone stopped them.

"Oh, yes!" Martha was saying. "George has a whole cabinet full of coins upstairs. I don't know what on earth he is going to do with them all. He just keeps collecting them and putting them into folders and jars and things. He spends hours at it. I wanted him to put them into a bank vault or some other safe place, but he wouldn't hear of it, said a hobby was not a hobby unless you could lay your hands on it." She looked coyly over her glasses at George. "Personally, I think the whole thing is rather silly."

She clapped her hand over her mouth, looked quickly at the two men, then drew her hand away. "Oh, goodness!" she tittered. "Maybe I shouldn't have said that, about it being silly, I mean. Maybe you two gentlemen are coin collectors too. Are you?"

Blackie exchanged glances with Wilber. "Yes," he said. "You could call us that."

The lines of peace which habitually marked George's lean face had vanished, and his lips had become thin and white with fear and anger. He had prepared himself for this—the gun on the cabinet in the kitchen, the rifle in the corner of the bedroom, the little automatic in the coin cabinet—and now he realized how futile his efforts had been. The guns were all in the wrong places. The rifle should be in the stairway, at his back, where he could lay his hands on it. He considered making a quick dash up the stairs to the bedroom, clutching up the rifle—

But that would leave Martha at their mercy! No, the rifle was out of the question. That left only the little automatic among the coins. If they would permit him to reach that cabinet, a flick of the safety, a touch of the trigger—

"We also collect guns," said Wilber. He slid a short-snouted .38 from the pocket of his coat and pointed it casually in George's direction.

George felt a spasm clutch his stomach at sight of

the thing. He wondered how many lives it had taken, how many more it would take.

"Oh, my!" Martha gasped. "I don't like guns! They frighten me half to death! But—but George collects them, too, like he does everything else. And I don't know why. He just keeps them lying around the house one in the kitchen, one in the bedroom, one in his coin cabinet. I've been after him time and time again to put them away."

George groaned inwardly. There went his last chance, his *only* chance! Martha had babbled it away without even realizing it.

He felt infinitely sorry for her. She seemed not to have the slightest notion as to what was going on. These men intended to kill her. They wore no masks; they'd leave no witnesses. They were murderers! And she was chatting on, entertainingly, about whatever entered her head, as if they were old friends who had just dropped in for tea.

"I do hope it isn't loaded," said Martha, drawing back another step from Wilber. "I don't like loaded guns. They're too dangerous. I keep telling George he shouldn't have loaded guns about the house. What if children should come in and get hold of one? Why, they could hurt themselves real bad. That's why I had all the bullets taken out of George's guns. Better be safe than sorry, I always say."

"Smart lady! Smart lady!" said Wilber, his thick lips twisting mockingly.

"Yes," said Blackie. *"Very!"*

"And now," said Wilber, getting up from the arm of the chair, "I think we had better have a look at your collection." He gathered up the two valises with one hand and made a slight motion with his gun toward the stairs. "Your coin collection, I mean."

George hesitated. The gun in Wilber's hand was less than three feet from him. If he made a sudden grab for it—

Then he felt the man's eyes upon him, saw the cold,

wary glint of them, and he knew he wouldn't stand a chance. He turned slowly and started up the stairs, his legs rubbery beneath him. He felt beaten, inadequate, utterly helpless.

"I wouldn't touch one of the things myself," Martha was chattering on. "That's why I had Brother Al unload them the last time he was here. When George was away, of course."

George paused on the stairs, felt the gun prod into the small of his back, then continued up the stairs.

"I do believe I have some cake left," Martha said to Blackie. "I'll bring you some and get you some cold milk to drink while they're looking at the collection." She started toward the kitchen.

Blackie stepped in front of her. "Don't bother," he said, dropping his right hand into his coat pocket. "Just stay here. And shut up!"

"I always try to have cake or cookies or something like that on hand," Martha explained. "Just in case someone should drop in. But we don't have many callers, living out here away from things as we are."

Blackie was trying not to listen to her. He had his attention tuned to the room above them. Twice he nodded his head in satisfaction as he heard the continued, muffled clinking of many coins being poured into a valise.

Martha heard it, too. "Maybe Mr. Wilber is buying the collection," she said. "I do hope so! George has been collecting for nearly twenty years. He must have thousands and thousands of all kinds of coins. And he spends so much time with them. Always sorting them and such. Why, some days I hardly get to talk with him at all."

Martha broke off. Blackie stiffened. The two shots from upstairs had come in rapid succession, startling abrupt.

Blackie's hand came swiftly from his pocket, bringing a gun with it. He brushed her aside, took a step nearer the stairs, and paused.

There was a sound of shuffling footsteps above. They faltered, approached the stairs, then dragged heavily as they came slowly down, step by step.

Blackie shoved Martha roughly against the wall, then stepped back, his gun covering both her and the doorway. "It had better be the right one," he said, thinly.

The footsteps paused, then came on again. George appeared in the doorway, his face sickly white. He was slumped over, nearly double, both hands clasping his stomach, his fingers crimson.

A piercing cry came from Martha's pale lips as she leaped toward him.

Blackie's hand tightened about the gun.

George staggered sideways through the door to the near wall, leaned his head against it.

Blackie relaxed, lowered his gun, and grinned. "Looks like you've had it, buddy," he said.

George began to slump lower along the wall. He reached out with his left hand toward Martha, clawed empty air, and lurched in front of her. Then his right hand swung suddenly out and around, and the little automatic in it spoke rapidly, three times.

A look of surprise chased the grin from Blackie's face a second or two before he hit the floor.

George had his arms around Martha, and she was struggling away from him. "You're hurt!" she screamed. "George, you're hurt!"

"It isn't my blood," he said, letting her free herself. "It belongs to the one upstairs. I had to use it to make my act look convincing."

Then she was in his arms again, and he was holding her tightly, feeling the warmth of her body slowly calming the cold sickness that was churning within him.

"They believed you," he whispered. "About the guns being unloaded. It threw Wilber off his guard— gave me the scant second I needed, *the scant second I had to have!*"

"After I finally realized who they were, I knew they would be watching you," she said, "watching your every move. I had to throw them off—somehow."

He relaxed his arms from about her and turned toward the telephone. Then he paused and turned back. "You know," he said, "you had *me* believing it, too— until that bit about some unknown character named Brother Al."

"I didn't know what else to do," said Martha. "I hoped you'd get the message."

"Smart lady! Smart lady!" said George, turning again toward the telephone.

"Yes," she said, pushing her glasses up to the bridge of her nose again. *"Very!"*

WELCOME
STRANGER

by Elijah Ellis

Three miles beyond the town Garvin slowed down and muttered disgustedly. He glanced again at the rear-view mirror of his sports car. There was only a battered old sedan behind him. Garvin turned his head slightly, and said, "He must have turned off somewhere."

Though to all appearances Garvin was alone in the car, a muffled voice answered from the closed luggage compartment just behind the seat. "That's funny. Way you talked, I thought we had a bite for sure."

"So did I," Garvin said. He frowned ahead along the narrow, multi-patched blacktop highway. "Well, I'll go on a few miles, then turn around. We'll give the town another try. Okay?"

"Okay, but don't take all day. It's hot in here, and I've got cramps on top of my cramps."

"Take it easy." Garvin laughed. He fed gas to the rakish, bright yellow car. It roared ahead. The small tape recorder in the inside breast pocket of his jacket was digging into his ribs, and he unbuttoned the jacket to ease the pressure. He lit a cigarette, flicked the match out the window.

As Mac, the man hidden in the luggage compartment, had said, it was strange that the black-and-white police car that had got on their tail back in the town had evidently given up the chase. That didn't square at all with the information they had about the endearing habits of the local-yokel lawmen of the town, Keysburg.

Garvin and Mac had heard from many sources that Keysburg had one of the most efficient setups for plucking suckers in the entire state. "Speed trap" was putting it mildly.

Consider the traffic light in the center of the tiny burg. The light was carefully concealed behind a sign-studded telephone pole. Then there was the "school crossing" sign hidden in a clump of weeds on a vacant lot bordering the highway, and the sign that announced in huge black letters, "20 MPH"; and just above it in microscopic type, "Minimum Speed."

Garvin tossed away his cigarette, and suddenly that nondescript old sedan that had been trailing him was alongside, and cutting in front. Garvin hit the brakes, swerved toward the ditch. The sports car skidded to a stop with its front wheels balanced precariously on the ditch's steep edge. Garvin sat there shaking.

Mac gargled, "What in the flaming . . ."

"Idiot forced me off the road," Garvin said, when he was able to talk. Then, looking ahead, he added, "Huh oh."

The sedan had stopped, and one of the two men inside it climbed out slowly. The afternoon sun winked on a silver badge pinned to the man's khaki shirt.

As the man ambled back toward the sports car, Garvin flicked on the tape recorder in his pocket. He murmured to Mac, "Maybe we got a bite, after all."

The man came on slowly, eyeing the out-of-state tag on Garvin's front bumper. Garvin blustered, "What you trying to do, Mister?"

"Better question—what're you tryin' to do?" the man drawled. He was tall and stoop-shouldered, and carried an outsized pistol slung low on one hip. "Kind of in a rush, ain't you, cuz?"

Garvin pretended to notice the badge for the first time, and said ingratiatingly, "Why, no, officer."

"Ashley's the name. County constable." He stared down at Garvin through pale gray eyes. "We got laws here about speedin' within the city limits."

Garvin blinked. "City? Why, Keysville is three or four miles back."

"It's Keys*burg*," Ashley said. He gave a wintry laugh. He pointed a forefinger at a hill far in the distance. "That there ridge marks the city limits. Kind of a spread-out town we got. I might overlook the speedin', since you're a stranger and all. We might even let you off with a warnin' for runnin' the traffic light in town, and ignorin' several signs. But we just can't put up with litterbugs."

"Litterbug?" Garvin said weakly.

Constable Ashley nodded slowly. "Oh, yes, cuz. I seen you throw out that smoulderin' cigarette. An' the match. An' a pile of newspapers, an' no tellin' what else."

Garvin felt a reluctant admiration. "Well, I . . ."

Ashley stiffened. "Oh? Threatenin' an officer, huh? That'll cost you, cuz."

"Why, I didn't . . ."

"The scout car officers back in town told me over the radio that you had a mean look about you—asked me and my partner to keep an eye on you. Lucky we did, I reckon. Can't be too careful."

"Constable, I didn't say any . . ."

"Shut that smart mouth, cuz." Ashley turned his head, called toward the other car, "Go on, Lem. I'll foller you."

The old sedan moved off down the highway, trailing a cloud of exhaust smoke.

Ashley snapped at Garvin, "Git over, cuz. I'll drive."

"Now just a moment," Garvin said. He hesitated. "What if I handed you a twenty, say?"

Ashley lifted a horny hand, slapped Garvin across the mouth. "Attempted brib'ry—that'll cost you, cuz. Git over."

Garvin got over. He rubbed his stinging lips. He swallowed his temper and whined, "I didn't mean anything."

Silently the constable got in under the wleel. He got the sports car back on the highway, then tramped on the gas. The car took off with a screech of tires. Within seconds they had passed the old sedan.

"Don't these speed laws apply to you?" Garvin muttered.

Ashley took his hand from the wheel long enough to slap Garvin again. "I ain't goin' to warn you again."

With an effort Garvin unclenched his fists, huddled down in the seat with an air of, he hoped, cringing apprehension. He touched the whirring tape recorder hidden in his jacket pocket. He thought, *Just wait, Cuz. Just wait.*

The sports car sailed over a hill. In the valley beyond, Ashley hit the brakes, careened off the highway onto a dusty, rutted lane. There was a ramshackle house up ahead, crouched in the middle of a straggling grove of trees.

Ashley stopped near the tumbledown front porch of the house. There was a faded sign on the wall of the house, near the door.

" 'Justice of the Peace,' " Garvin read aloud.

"That's right, cuz. Get out."

Garvin opened his door. He started to slide out.

Suddenly the constable put a palm against his back and shoved, hard. Garvin sprawled to his hands and knees.

"Tryin' to escape, huh? That'll cost you, cuz."

The other car came along the lane, stopped across the yard. A carbon copy of Constable Ashley got out and strolled forward.

Ashley told him, "Feller tried to make a run for it, Lem."

"I seen him," Lem said, with a chuckle. "Mean as hell."

"Judge'll take care of him," Ashley said.

Lem nodded, watching Garvin get painfully to his feet. Now a large, potbellied man shambled out of the house. He frowned at Garvin. His tiny eyes moved on to the expensive sports car, the out-of-state tag. The frown gave way to an anticipatory beam. "Well now."

"Sho'," Ashley said, "got us a real bad 'un."

"Bring him in," the judge rumbled. He led the way into a dim, shabbily furnished room, and lowered his bulk into a chair behind an ancient desk. "Ah?" he said.

"Town boys tipped us to this feller on the radio," Ashley explained. "They had about half-a-dozen charges on him, a'fore he got out of town. Then we picked him up, and lordy! Speedin', litterin' the highway, reckless drivin', attempted brib'ry . . ."

"Just a minute," the judge broke in. He whacked his pudgy knuckles on the desk top, cleared his throat, and said, "Court's now in session. Go ahead, Constable."

"Interferin' with a officer doin' his duty, attempted assault, an' as you can see, Judge, the feller is fallin' down drunk." Ashley paused for breath.

The judge nodded ponderously. He rubbed a hand over the bald expanse of his skull. "Well, now," he said comfortably. Then his gimlet eyes turned to Garvin. "Got anythin' important to say?"

"Why, this is highway robbery," Garvin sputtered. "It's insane. All of those so-called charges, none of them true. I've heard rumors about this place. But I'd never have believed . . ."

"Uh huh," the judge said. He smiled. "Contempt of court. Want to go on?"

Garvin threw up his hands. "Alright. How much?"

The judge scribbled on a piece of paper. Ashley and Lem watched him breathlessly. Garvin sent a quick glance toward the open door. He knew Mac would be just outside, drinking in every word. And the tape recorder in Garvin's pocket would have it all down, loud and clear. He smiled.

"Ha, well," the judge said, finally, "I figger that comes to something like two hundred dollars."

The three men looked toward Garvin. He didn't have to pretend a shudder. "That's . . ."

"That's it," the judge growled. "Two hundred dollars, or two hundred days in jail. Take your pick."

Garvin fumbled out his wallet, let it drop to the floor. He bent down, but Ashley was ahead of him. The lanky constable straightened with the wallet in his hands. He riffled through a fat sheaf of bills.

"Judge, he's got a roll here'd choke a horse."

The judge shoved out his hand. "Gimme." He took the wallet from Ashley, peered inside. He whistled softly. Then he cleared his throat, and said, "On second thought, Mister, I'm afraid your fine will be a little more. I overlooked a couple of things while ago. Let's say three hundred dollars."

"You want me to pay you three hundred dollars?" Garvin said slowly and distinctly.

"You heard him, cuz," Ashley snapped.

"And you're gettin' off easy," the judge said.

The other constable, Lem, said, "Why don't we take it all? What the heck? This feller ain't goin' to do nothin' about it. What he could do?"

Silence. Then the judge murmured, "I think you have a point there, Lem."

And that was plenty. More than plenty, Garvin told himself in grim triumph. He backed toward the door, getting well clear of any reaching arms. Then he pulled the tape recorder from his pocket, snapped it off. He waggled it at the three men.

"What's that thing?" Lem asked.

"A nice little gadget that's going to put you thieves behind bars for a long, long time," Garvin said crisply.

Ashley stammered, "Listen here, you can't pull . . ."

"Oh, yes, I can—cuz," Garvin told him. "Every word you crooks have said is here on tape. All the hoked-up charges. And most especially, that last little bit about taking all my money. Eh, Judge?"

The judge's fat face gleamed with sweat. "Who are you?"

"Throw me that wallet, quick," Garvin said. And, when he had it, he flipped it open to the cardcase. He let them see an official-looking card. "State crime bureau," he said shortly. "Satisfied?"

"Oh, lordy," Lem wheezed.

Ashley looked as if he might faint.

The judge opened and shut his mouth like a fish out of water, finally managed, "Well, now. Maybe we can do business."

"What are you suggesting?" Garvin said.

Taking a small key from his pants pocket, the judge shakily unlocked the desk. He brought out a small metal box. From it he drew fat wads of money. "There's about two-thousand here."

"Tryin' to bribe an officer, eh?" Garvin mocked.

"Come on, let's be serious about this," the judge said.

"I'm plenty serious." Garvin jerked his head toward the door. "Let's go, boys. There's a cell waiting for you, up at Capitol City."

Now the judge had found another metal box, containing another hoard. "Three thousand," he groaned. Huge beads of sweat rolled down his jowls.

"How long did it take you to collect that?" Garvin asked. "How many poor slobs did you and your goons here rob in this kangaroo court?"

The judge waved his hands bitterly. "Skip the sermon."

For the past few seconds, Ashley had been easing behind Lem. Now Ashley suddenly jerked out his gun, leaped toward Garvin, thrusting the big .45 ahead of him.

"You fool!" Ashley cried. "You think we'd just let you haul us off to jail like a bunch of sheep?"

Garvin said calmly, "Look over by the door, cuz."

Mac stood framed in the doorway, with a gun trained on the constable's head. With a frightened bleat, Ashley dropped his .45, and hurriedly backed away.

' "You want to try, Lem?" Garvin asked.

Lem's gun thudded to the floor. "Not me, Mister."

While Mac covered the three, Garvin stepped to the desk, scooped up the money, stuffed it into his pockets, making a prominent bulge.

"I'm going to give you boys a break you don't deserve," Garvin said. He turned, walked to the door.

Behind him, the judge said, "How about that tape?"

Garvin didn't bother to answer. Seconds later he and Mac were speeding toward the highway. Mac glanced back.

"Whew!" Mac said. "They didn't follow us out. I was afraid they would. What a way to make a living!"

Garvin turned the car onto the highway. He laughed shakily. "Yeah, but look at the short hours and the long pay."

Several minutes and several miles later, Mac asked, "Think they really believed you were a state cop?"

Garvin shrugged. "Well, that old Army I.D. card does look pretty official. You know something? I've a good mind to put that tape we have in a little box, and send it to the state cops—the real ones, I mean. Of all the dirty crooks I ever saw, those three are the worst."

Mac nodded hesitantly. "One thing, though, before you send that tape anywhere."

"Yeah?"

"Just be sure you wipe off any fingerprints that might be on it."

"Yeah."

COME RIDE WITH ME

by Donald Honig

With the exception of an occasional farmhouse set back in the rolling hills, the only lights for miles around belonged to the Quick Stop roadside diner. The flashing neon light beat on and off rhythmically, lurid and persistent in the night.

The lone man walking along the side of the highway had been watching the sign for some time, his eyes fixed upon it. Despite the night's chill air he was walking slowly, contemplating that sign with a dim, faraway look in his eyes. Wearing a parka, the hood thrown back, his hands were deep in the slit pockets on either side of the jacket. The fingers of his right hand were fondling a .38 revolver.

When he came within several hundred feet of the diner, Gannon stopped. He studied the three cars parked under the blinking neon sign, none of them belonging to the police. Having satisfied himself on this point, Gannon moved on again. He approached the diner slowly, a cool, hostile look in his eyes as he peered through the diner's windows at the men sitting at the counter. They all seemed preoccupied, as people in lonely eating places late at night generally do.

Gannon mounted the steps and went in. The men at the counter looked up at him for a moment, then turned their faces back to the plates in front of them. The place was quiet, except for the country ballads coming softly from the radio.

Gannon settled himself on a stool at the end of the counter, away from the other men. He folded his hands on the counter top and sidled a glance at the other customers.

Three cars were parked outside, three men at the counter. Each of the men had a shabby, rural look—rough clothing, sallow weather-beaten faces. None of those automobiles outside was much of a bargain either, but then Gannon couldn't have expected much more, given where he was.

The counterman, bald, with a frank, smiling face, approached him. "Didn't hear you drive up," he said. "What can we do for you?"

"Just coffee."

"That'll do it?"

"Very nicely," Gannon said.

When the man had gone to draw the coffee, Gannon bent his head and gazed down into his folded hands. Sitting, he realized how tired he was. He had been walking for hours. He was going to get himself a car now, no matter how beat up it was. He was tired of walking and, more importantly, he had to get out of this area; that was the paramount thing.

The counterman returned with the coffee and set it down. "Something else?" he asked. "Piece of pie?"

"Nothing else," Gannon said, and the man went away.

The country ballads were gone from the radio now and the news was coming on. Gannon brought the coffee to his lips and fixed his eyes expectantly on the radio, as though it were about to address him directly. The announcer began talking about a man who had earlier that day attempted to rob a supermarket. A young clerk had tried to foil the holdup and been shot dead. The holdup man—murderer, now—had escaped on foot. All persons in the area were warned to be on the lookout for him. Motorists were cautioned against picking up hitchhikers.

Then the announcer read a description of the wanted man, sending it out through the night into the livingrooms and kitchens of the scattered farmhouses, into automobiles on the road, and into the brightly lit interior of the Quick Stop diner.

Curiously, almost critically, Gannon listened. They had his age guessed correctly, within a year; the color of his hair was slightly wrong; his height and weight were approximately right; and of course they mentioned the parka, which was still on his back.

Gannon put his cup down and looked at the other men. None seemed to have paid attention to the broadcast. The three heads were stlll bent over their plates, the three jaws working in unison. The counterman was scraping the griddle with a spatula. The broadcast had come and gone. The tension Gannon had felt during the broadcast began to subside. He resumed sipping his coffee, holding the warm cup in both hands.

At the sound of a car entering the diner's lot, Gannon turned his head. This was what he had been hoping for—a big, powerful, late-model car. Give him that and he could break through any roadblocks that might have been set up down the highway.

A man got out of the car and hurried toward the diner. He was in his mid-thirties, well-dressed, and Gannon especially noted the man's topcoat; that would be much better than the damned parka, which everybody knew about now.

When the man entered the diner, the counterman said, "Hello, Lee."

The man didn't answer. He seemed agitated, and headed for the phone booth on the far side of the diner, the leather heels of his shoes clicking on the tile.

Gannon got up, dropped a quarter onto the counter and quietly left.

Outside, he headed straight for that appealing car. Nearing it, he looked back over his shoulder, but no one in the diner was paying any attention to him. Gannon opened the back door of the car, got in, closed the door behind him and crouched in the dark, pressing himself against the front seat. His right hand was deep in the pocket of his parka, clutching the .38.

He waited. The minutes passed. He began to wonder if the man had sat down for a meal. Nevertheless, he kept his head down. He was patient. He had time. He could wait.

After about fifteen minutes, Gannon heard those leather heels clicking across the paved parking lot. Then the front door opened, the dome light flashed on for a moment but went off as the door slammed shut. The engine started with a smooth hum. The car, however, lurched out of the parking lot with a jack-rabbit start that threw Gannon against the back seat.

The car picked up speed, racing along the highway. Gannon waited for several minutes, a smirk on his face. Then he drew the .38 from his pocket and slowly rose in the dark. The man behind the wheel did not immediately notice him.

"All right," Gannon said.

The man was startled, his shoulders jerking forward, his head twitching around.

"Keep your eye on the road," Gannon said. "This thing you feel against your head is a .38 revolver."

"Who the hell are you?" the man demanded, his voice brusque, angry.

"I'm the man who's going to borrow your car," Gannon said. "You'll slow down when I tell you to."

"You must be the guy they were talking about on the radio," the man said, his eyes flicking in and out of the rear-view mirror.

"That's right," Gannon said. "So you do just as I tell you and don't try to be a boy scout."

"Do you know who that was who was just in here?" the counterman was saying to his customers. "That was Lee Carstair."

"That was him?" one of the men said.

"Sure was," the counterman said. "He's livin' in a beehive, that boy."

"Why so?" another man asked.

"You ain't heard?" the counterman asked. "Why, Lee got caught embezzlin' money from his father-in-law's company. The old man fired him last week, and now I heard the wife's left him, and the old man is goin' to press charges. That was the old man he was telephonin' just now. I heard him say the name."

"From all the shoutin'," one of the men said, "I guess Lee didn't hear what he wanted to hear."

The counterman laughed. "No sirree. That boy's got problems high as a mountain."

"Slow down, I say!" Gannon shouted. "Slow down, damn you, or I'll kill you!"

Lee Carstair laughed hysterically. The car was barreling along the highway at 90 miles an hour.

"What are you doing?" Gannon screamed.

"You picked the wrong guy," Carstair yelled.

They came to a long curve around a rock wall where the highway had been blasted through. Carstair lifted his hands from the wheel and covered his face.

"Oh, God," he said softly, allowing the hurtling car to smash itself furiously into the rocks.

SHERIFF PEAVY'S
COSA NOSTRA CAPER

by Richard Hardwick

Deputy Jerry Sealey was in high gear when he bolted through the office door and stopped in front of Sheriff Dan Peavy's desk. After catching his breath, he posed a rhetorical question, "Guess who's payin' Guale County a visit!"

Without moving his feet off the desk or opening his eyes, Dan said, "Khrushchev," his expression placid.

"Funny, funny!" Jerry snorted. "But it might be a lot worse than Khrushchev!" He glanced around at me, rocked back on his heels the way he does when big things are in the wind, and said, "None other than Johnny Cadillac himself!"

I stopped what I was doing, which was filing away the week's paper work. Dan Peavy's prune-textured face was still in complete repose, but one eyelid lifted slowly, and he pushed a hand through his wild thatch of white hair. "Johnny *what?*"

"Cadillac! *Ca*dillac!" Jerry shouted. "Ain't you ever heard of Johnny *Cadillac?*"

"Is he on teevee?" Dan inquired.

"Pete . . ." Jerry said to me in exasperation. "You've heard of him, ain't you?"

I nodded. "Dan, if it's true we better find out."

"Whataya mean, *if* it's true?" Jerry exploded, his thin form bending toward me as he knuckled down on Dan's desk. "I seen him with my own two eyes!"

Weathering the outburst, I went on. "Dan, we oughta find out what he's doing here. This fella's a big time hoodlum from up east."

"You can say that again!" Jerry affirmed. "One of the roughest guys around, and up to his eyeballs in that Cosa Nostra outfit."

Dan got up and walked over to the water cooler. "You say you seen him?"

"Right! I was comin' back into town on the Kingston Road and stopped off at the Midway Motel. The new owner, Kemper, usually keeps a pot o' coffee goin', and when I went inside he said he wanted me to see something in the registration book. Well, sir, there it was in this big scrawl—Johnny Cadillac, New York City! And he signed up for rooms for two people with him, Ramona Locke and E. Moran. Then Kemper took me over to the window and pointed out to the swimmin' pool. 'That's him,' he said. 'That's Johnny Cadillac!' "

"E. Moran?" I queried. "I wonder if that might be 'Ears' Moran?"

Jerry slapped his forehead and straight-armed a finger at me. "I'll just bet it *is!*"

Dan crumpled his paper cup and tossed it into the waste basket. "Say this fella's a real big gangster, huh?" he said, coming back to the desk. "Since you already got a look at him, Jerry, you stay here and get a wire off to the FBI, see if he's wanted any place. Pete, let's me and you run out to the motel and have a chat with him."

On the way, I filled Dan Peavy in as best I could on the notorious Johnny Cadillac. "The stuff I've read about him ties him in with all kinds of rackets, from extortion to bookmaking, and a good bit of larceny thrown in. And Ears Moran, if that's the guy with him, is sort of a sidekick of Cadillac's."

When we arrived at the Midway Motel we found Kemper huddled nervously behind the counter, as if he expected a bomb to go off momentarily. I asked him which room was Johnny Cadillac's.

"It's No. 5," he said. "But he ain't in it. He's right out there by the pool, same as he was when Jerry was here." He indicated an olive-skinned individual with shiny black hair. The man wore bathing trunks and was reading a newspaper. "Sheriff Peavy . . ." Kemper went on hesitantly. "There ain't gonna be any trouble, is there? No . . . no gunplay?"

Dan gave him a sour look and tapped me on the arm. As we walked out toward the pool I felt a bit of the apprehension the motel manager had expressed.

Cadillac looked up as we approached. His eyes dropped to the badge adorning Dan's khaki shirt, and he got to his feet. "Well, well!" he said, flashing a big, toothy smile. "If it ain't the law!"

"That's right, Mr. Lincoln," said Dan.

The smile twisted down slightly at the corners. "Cadillac's the name. You know, like the car."

"Sorry," Dan replied. "I'm Sheriff Peavy, and this here's Deputy Miller. Been hearin' some tales about you, Mr. Cadillac. You visitin' Guale County on business or pleasure?"

"Why, pleasure, Sheriff. Here, have a seat." He said expansively, pulling a couple of aluminum chairs up beside his. "You too, deputy." He stepped to one side, cupped a hand to his mouth and yelled toward the office: *"Hey!* You in there! Get a couple of beers out here for my pals! *Pronto!"*

"Yes, sir, Mr. Cadillac," came Kemper's immediate and quavering reply.

"Never mind that," said Dan. "Now back to what you're doin' here . . ."

"Hold on just a minute, Sheriff," he interrupted. "Hey, Goldie! C'mere!" This time he was yelling at a woman who had been splashing around in the shallow end of the pool. She climbed out and came toward us, hips wiggling like she was coming down a runway. She was very well put together, but even from this distance I could see the years were beginning to gain ground here and there.

"Meet Sheriff Levy and his deputy," said Johnny Cadillac. "This is my fiancée, Miss Goldie Locke."

"Ma'am," Dan said with a nod, and then added, somewhat chastened, "The name's Peavy."

"Pleased to meetcha, I'm sure," said Miss Locke.

"I was just telling the sheriff we're here on a little vacation, baby." He took a deep breath and thumped his chest. "Fishing, swimming, sunshine, the simple back-to-nature life. Nothing like this back in the city."

Goldie shifted her weight to her other hip. "Johnny, maybe they know him."

Cadillac gave his ear a thoughtful tug. "Yeah—this pal of ours said for us to be sure and say hello to Ed Allen while we was down here. Maybe you could tell us where to find him."

Dan shook his head slowly. "Can't say I know no Ed Allen. You, Pete?"

I mulled it over. "Well, there's Horace Allen runs the Guale Inn out at the beach, and old Judd Allen that's got a hog ranch up in the north part of the county . . ."

"Don't sound like the one we're looking for, does it, Goldie?" Johnny Cadillac said with a sudden hard tone to his voice, though the smile stayed plastered on.

She bit her lip. "N . . . no, Johnny, it don't. But maybe they just don't know him."

"And maybe you got the wrong name, baby." He took hold of her arm. "You wouldn't do that, would you?"

Kemper came sprinting across the lawn with a tray bearing several bottles of beer. He put them down on the metal table beside the chairs. "Anything else, sir?"

Cadillac picked up his shirt, pulled a bill out of the pocket and handed it to Kemper. "Beat it."

"Where's your friend?" Dan asked. "Mr. Moran?"

"Ears? Go get him, Goldie."

"He's taking a nap, honey. He drove all the way, remember, and he's dog tired—"

"I said get him, baby. Now."

This man had a great command of tones of voice. There was no doubt whatsoever, just from the way he said it, that dire things would happen if Goldie made any further protest. She hurried off toward the motel.

"Sheriff," Johnny Cadillac said, "where can I buy me a good boat around here?"

"There's Frye's Hardware and Marine in town," I told him. "And maybe you can pick up a used one at the county marina."

"Just for fishin'?" Dan inquired.

Cadillac looked him in the eye. "That's right. For fishing."

Dan gave his lumpy nose a little pull. "Best way for a stranger to fish is to hire a guide. There's half a dozen fishin' camps around the county."

The woman was coming back, and trailing along behind her, yawning and rubbing his bald head, was a dumpy little man in Bermuda shorts and a T shirt.

"Meet my pal, Ears Moran, Sheriff," Johnny Cadillac said.

Ears frowned darkly. "Whatsa beef, Johnny? What's with the fuzz?"

"No beef, you jerk! Just a sociable call."

Dan Peavy glanced at each of them, his eyes stopping on the leader. "I reckon you might call it that. Just want you folks to understand Guale County is a peaceful place, and we aim to keep it that way."

Johnny Cadillac threw an arm around each of his companions, the swarthy face broadening into a wider grin than before. "Sheriff, you're looking at the peace-lovingest folks you'll ever meet."

"What do you figure, Dan?" I asked as we headed back into town.

"Dunno. Couldn't hardly be hidin' out." He stared out the window for a while. "I wonder what that business about Ed Allen was all about?"

"Whatever it was, he sure wasn't very happy to find we didn't know the guy."

"We'll just have to keep a close eye on 'em. See what happens."

When we reached the office Jerry was standing outside on the sidewalk. He was talking, even before I could get the car stopped.

"We're in for something big, Dan!" he yelled excitedly. "Something mighty big! Horace Allen just phoned in from the Guale Inn said some real shady-lookin' characters just rented one of his cabins. He told me the names they signed, and you'll never guess who they are!"

"No more guessin' games, Jerry," Dan said tiredly as we trooped into the office.

"Well, it's more gangsters—three of 'em. Blinky Allegro, Seven-Finger Norton, and J. Edward Jones! I tell you, this could be another Appalachia."

I didn't keep tabs on the big-league underworld as closely as Jerry did, but when Dan glanced at me for confirmation, I had to admit I had heard of Blinky and Seven-Finger. "I don't know about Jones," I added, "but if he's with 'em, that's enough for me."

"Jerry," said the sheriff, "you get that wire off to the FBI on the first bunch?"

"Right."

"Okay. Pete, you stay here and wire 'em about the new ones." He motioned to Jerry. "Let's go, Deputy. Guale Inn. No time to waste."

The reply on Johnny Cadillac and company came in about five minutes before Dan and Jerry got back to the office. The wire said that the trio was not wanted at present, but they would bear watching, and that transcripts of their records were being forwarded.

The interview with Norton, Allegro, and Jones had panned out almost exactly like the first one, according to Dan. They were on a vacation trip, the length of which was as yet undetermined; they planned to fish and relax, and the farthest thing from their thoughts was any sort of unpleasantness.

"But we don't swallow that!" Jerry snapped. "They're up to something."

"Sure they are," said Dan. "And they ain't dumb

enough to think we're dumb enough not to know it. But *what* are they up to?"

"I say we bring 'em in and give 'em a good grillin'," Jerry suggested.

"We'll see what their records show," Dan said sensibly. "Meantime, let's keep our eyes open."

I was crossing the street next morning to get a cup of coffee at the Bon Air Cafe, when I saw a big black car with New York plates pull up in front of Frye's Hardware and Marine on the next block. Johnny Cadillac, Goldie, and Ears got out and filed into the store, and I spun on my heel and trotted back to the office.

"Dan, the Midway Motel gang is down at Frye's right this minute!"

He went to the window, looked out at the black car, and gave his potato-like nose a twist. "Soon as they leave, Pete, you run down there and find out what they bought."

I went to the cafe and got my coffee. I was on my third cup when the big car pulled away from the curb and purred back in the direction of the motel. I slid a quarter across the counter. "Keep the change, Thelma."

"What change?" she yelled after me. "Coffee's a dime a cup!"

"Pay you later," I said, hurrying out.

When I walked into Frye's I saw a sight I did not recall ever having seen before. Old man Frye was smiling.

"Good morning, Deputy Miller!" he said cheerily. "What can I do for you?"

"Those folks that just left. Two men and a woman—"

"Wonderful folks, Pete. Nice, solid, cash customers."

"What'd they buy?" I asked him.

The query seemed to have about the same effect a good goose would have had. "What *didn't* they buy!" he exulted. "Here!" He picked up a sales ticket and handed it to me. "Look at this! And it was cash!"

Listed in the old man's meticulous handwriting was a sale which totalled over three thousand dollars. There was an eighteen-foot boat, a seventy-five horsepower outboard, assorted fishing tackle, bug spray, suntan lotion, boat accessories, camping equipment, navigation charts, three picks and three shovels. Plus sales tax.

I looked back at the price of the boat. "Is this one of those boats you've been stuck with—you've had for about a year?"

He rubbed his hands together briskly enough to produce smoke. "It is."

I stared at the price again. "But—this is about two hundred dollars more than you asked when you first got it!"

The smile vanished and he snatched the ticket from me. "Just leave the pricin' to me, Deputy."

I wondered how his little swindle would set if I told him who he had sold the stuff to. "They say anything about what they wanted the digging tools for?"

He shrugged. "They're goin' fishing, maybe they wanta dig worms. It's their business, not mine." Behind me the front doorbell jingled. " 'Scuse me. More customers."

I took another look at the sales ticket where he had put it back on the spindle. The fishing in Guale County wasn't *that* good. I decided a few more questions might turn something up, so I busied myself thumbing through a catalog.

"Some pals of ours was in here a while ago, Pop," I heard a bass voice saying. "What'd you sell 'em?"

"Friends of yours?" Frye asked.

"Come on, come on!" piped up an impatient tenor. "Two guys and a doll."

"Oh . . ." said Frye, "*those* friends."

There was nothing confidential about the purchase apparently, and while Frye ticked off the items, I looked around slowly and saw that there were three men listening intently to the information. A heavyset one with a square jaw struck a match, and holding a cigar to his mouth with one hand, touched the light to the end of it. There was something odd about the hands. The *fingers*—I counted them. Three on the left, four on the right. A little quick mental arithmetic, and I knew I was looking at the notorious 'Seven-Finger' Norton.

The short, oily character to his right, wearing heavy glasses, had to be Blinky Allegro. The third one, lacking any noticeable oddity, would be J. Edward Jones.

"Okay, Pop," said Seven-Finger, when Frye was done talking. "We want the same as our pals got. How much is it gonna cost?"

The old man reached back to support himself against a counter. He began stuttering, and finally managed, "It . . . you . . . comes to $3170. Can't possibly come out for less . . ."

Seven-Finger nudged the man to his left. "The dough, J. Ed."

Jones pulled out a fat wallet, licked his thumb, and began counting. He slapped the wad of bills down on the counter and rammed the wallet back into the pocket.

"Now then, Pop," said Seven-Finger, "when is Johnny's—our pal's stuff—gonna be ready to go?"

"Tomorrow—about noon . . ." croaked Frye.

"We'll pick ours up right after he leaves. And Pop, don't say nothing to our pals about us. We wanta surprise them." As one, they turned and marched out, climbed into another black sedan, and headed out toward the beach road.

Frye stood staring after them.

"Whatever they're up to," I said to Dan Peavy after reporting what I had learned at Frye's, "they won't be doing it till tomorrow afternoon."

The morning mail had come in while I was gone, and the police records of Johnny Cadillac and his two companions were on the desk. Dan had been going

over them. "You boys were right," he admitted.
"They're a pretty rough bunch." He handed me one of
the sheets. "Take a look here, Pete. Might be some
connection."

It was the record on Ramona Locke, alias Goldie
Locke. She had served a few short stretches here and
there over the past ten years, mostly little things. It
also said that she was the girl friend of one 'Bugs' Casino.

"That name Casino strikes a note with me," Dan
said. "Wasn't there something in the papers about him
not long ago?"

Jerry had come in and was reading over my shoulder. "That's right," he said. " 'Bugs' Casino died about
a month ago. He was in prison. Had some kinda accident, and died in the prison hospital. He was in for
that big armored car robbery about five or six years
ago. The dough never did turn up."

Dan Peavy hoisted his feet onto the desk and closed
his eyes. " 'Course, could just be a coincidence. Then
again, it might not be. Jerry, run down to the *Clarion*
office and get the news stories on that robbery."

'Bugs' Casino and two accomplices had decoyed an
armored money truck seven years ago, tied up the
guards, and made off with slightly over two million
dollars in cool cash. A lone fingerprint had identified
Casino. He was picked up a month later in California,
and though he admitted his part in the robbery, he
insisted his two pals had double-crossed him and made
off with the loot.

The most recent news item said that Casino, serving
a ten-year stretch for the robbery, was fatally injured
when a scaffold fell on him during some construction
in the prison library, where Casino was librarian. In
recapping, the item said that his accomplices in the big
robbery were never apprehended, and the money
never found.

"Now take a look at this," Jerry said triumphantly,
reading aloud from the clipping. "Miss Ramona

Locke, an exotic dancer identified as Casino's girl friend, was at the convict's bedside when death came the following day, ending a criminal career dating back . . ." He looked up at Dan and me. "Whatd'ya think of that!"

Dan Peavy nodded. "If he did stash some o' the loot, that would have been his last chance to tell somebody. But why the devil *here?* Guale County, of all places in . . ."

"It adds up, though," I said. "Boat, charts, all that stuff to dig with. And there's no law that says they can't ride around in a boat with picks and shovels."

"That explains Johnny Cadillac's bunch," said Jerry. "Now what about Seven-Finger Norton and his boys?"

"Probably got wind of what they were looking for and followed 'em down here," I suggested.

That night was Dan Peavy's chess night with Doc Stebbins, and when he left the office Jerry looked out the window to be sure he wasn't coming back, then turned toward me enthusiastically. "Pete, I did a little checkin' out at the motel this afternoon. Kemper said Cadillac's gang went into town for supper at about eight-thirty, and was gone more'n an hour. That'll give me and you plenty of time to—"

"Hold it!" I snapped. "Hold it right there! I'm pretty sure I know what you wanta do, and all I can say is not on your tintype, buddy! I ain't breaking into nobody's room with you or anybody else. You got to have a warrant for that kinda thing."

"Warrant, schmarrant," he squealed. "Besides, we ain't gonna *break* in." He pulled a key from his pocket and dangled it before me. "It's a master key. Got it from Kemper hisself. And we ain't gonna take nothing, Pete. All we want is some idea of where they think that money is. That way we could beat 'em to it. You said, yourself, that boat they bought ain't gonna be ready till noon tomorrow."

There was some vague logic in there somewhere,

and, when I didn't resume my opposition immediately, Jerry continued. "Look, Pete, our job is to uphold the law here and protect the citizens. Now, suppose these gangsters started one of them gang wars they're always startin', shooting machine guns up and down the street . . ." He waved his hand toward the street outside the window. "Them citizens out there are countin' on us, Pete, night and day."

Jerry's eloquent plea was spoiled only slightly by the fact that the only citizen in sight at the moment was Mac Snipes, one of our town's leading drunks.

"Are you sure about that dinner at eight-thirty business?" I asked.

"Come on! We'll see for ourselves!"

We were out of uniform and in Jerry's car. We parked on a little side road about a hundred yards from the motel, just as it was getting dark, and we made our way through the underbrush and took up a position behind a big live oak tree, directly across Kingston Road from the building. Sure enough, at exactly eight-thirty the three of them came out and climbed into the big black sedan and motored off towards town.

As the car vanished down the road, we scurried across to the motel and stopped at Room No. 5. Jerry took out the key, gave me a sly grin, and proceeded to unlock the door.

With last-minute misgivings, I said, "I ain't so sure about this idea . . ."

But the door was open and he pushed me inside. "We'll be outta here in five minutes, Pete," he said, easing the door shut. "Now quit worrying."

I looked around the room. It was an ordinary motel unit, maybe a bit larger than most, couple of double beds, dresser, chairs, bedtable, teevee on wheels, closet, and bathroom. There were clothes scattered around, newspapers 'all over, and ashtrays crammed with twisted-out butts. Two whiskey bottles stood on the dresser, along with half a dozen bottles of seltzer water.

"Ah ha!" Jerry said. "Look on the bed. We've hit the jackpot."

Lying there, partly covered by a shirt, was a chart. It was the U. S. Coast and Geodetic chart showing the coastal inlets and rivers of Guale and adjoining counties.

"Now we're getting somewhere!" said Jerry. But after making a careful examination of the chart and finding no markings that had not been put there by the printing press, it seemed that we were not really getting anywhere at all, for the chart covered an area of seven or eight hundred square miles.

"Maybe they *are* here to go fishing," I suggested.

"A guy like Johnny Cadillac don't give a hoot for fishing. Let's keep lookin'. Maybe we can find something else."

A sudden sound froze both of us. Someone was gently inserting a key in the lock on the door.

"Omigosh, Pete!" Jerry whispered in panic. *"They're back!"*

The only other possibility I could see was that it might be Kemper, the manager. But we couldn't risk it. "Quick! Get in the closet."

Jerry stood transfixed, staring saucer-eyed at the door that would be opening any second now. I grabbed his arm, shoved him into the closet, and closed the door behind us. It was fairly large as closets go, and I crammed Jerry down in one corner, squeezed down beside him, and took a blanket which was lying on the folding luggage rack and draped it over us. The same reasoning process probably goes through an ostrich's head in time of peril.

Outside, someone spoke in a satisfied voice. "I can work that kinda lock in my sleep, boss."

"Shut up and keep an eye at the window!" snapped a bass voice. "Get busy, J. Ed."

"Hey, boss!" said a tenor. "Here's a map."

Jerry whispered: "Pete . . . it's *them!* It's Seven-Finger Norton and his boys."

So we weren't the only ones interested in Johnny Cadillac and his friends. Very interesting, I thought, up to a point. That point being the moment they opened the closet door. I hoped I could say something appropriate and snappy before they shot us.

"We'll take the map with us," said Bass Voice.

"I'll check the closet, boss," said Tenor.

"Pete . . ." Jerry whimpered.

"Hold it!" there was a hasty rattling of Venetian blinds. "It's them, boss! Johnny's car just pulled in!"

"There ain't no back way outta these dumps," snapped Bass Voice. "Everybody into the closet quick!"

I heard the closet door open, and I clenched my teeth against the coming explosion and the bullet ripping through my innocent and far-too-young-to-die body.

"Get a move on, J. Ed! They're at the door!" There was much grunting and cursing, and then the door was closed. Someone pushed the luggage rack hard against us. They were all three in the other corner, not two feet from us. I could hear them breathing and squirming around to get situated.

"Get your rods ready, boys," whispered Bass Voice. "If they open this door, let Johnny have it first."

"Right, boss."

"Check, boss."

"Get that damned gun outta my ear!"

"Sorry, boss."

"*Shhhh!*"

I realized suddenly that that had been Jerry! But each of our fellow occupants must have thought it was one of the others, because they quieted down. And none too soon, judging from the footsteps on the other side of the closet door.

"Why couldn't we eat in town, Johnny?" That was Goldie, petulant.

"I said we'd eat here because I can think better with a little privacy. Open them sandwiches up, Ears. Now then, Goldie, take it right from when you first seen him. I want the whole thing, every last word."

"But we been through it a dozen times . . ."

"Every word, Goldie. Got that?" Hard, cold.

"Sure . . . Johnny. Well, when they told 'Bugs' he was dying, he said he wanted to see me, and the warden called me. So I went to the prison hospital and there was poor Bugs all wrapped up in bandages and one leg up in a sling and—"

Whap! "The talk, stupid. The *talk.*"

"I'm getting to it, Johnny!" she wailed. "You didn't have to slug me."

"You want mustard, Johnny?"

"Shut up, bird-brain! Go on, Goldie."

"Well, poor 'Bugs' tried to smile through all that tape and gauze, and he said 'Hi, doll' in this weak voice. I sat down by the bed, and the copper went and stood at the door. I leaned down to hear what 'Bugs' was trying to say. I tell you, I was about to bust out crying. His mouth moved and he said . . ."

"You dint say about the mustard, Johnny," persisted Ears, drowning out Goldie for a moment.

". . . 'the big dough . . . buried . . . in Georgia . . .' and then he started coughing like he'd never stop. The copper asked if I wanted him to call the doc, and 'Bugs' gave his head a little shake, like there wasn't time for that. He was holding my hand and he squeezed it and I leaned down again. He was trying real hard to say something, his mouth going like a fish outta water. He was hurting my hand he squeezed so hard, and then his eyes kinda rolled up in his head . . ." Her voice broke and she began to sob.

"How about catsup, Johnny?"

Goldie tried to go on rather than risk another rap in the mouth. "And he whispered 'See Ed Allen,' or it coulda been 'Eddie Allen.' He was gasping like, and hard to understand, and then his whole body sorta

pushed up offa the bed and he . . . and he whispered
my name and his . . . like he meant we'd be together
always . . . and then he . . . then he *died!*" She was
wailing like a siren by this time, and I could hear
somebody walking up and down, probably Johnny
Cadillac.

"You still ain't said about the mustard and catsup—"

Cadillac loosed a string of curses. "If you wasn't my
sister's husband, Ears, I'd kick your stupid head in!
Shut up so's I can think!"

"Yeah," mumbled Ears. "Maybe I'll have a drink,
too. Them burgers is cold anyhow."

"It's this Allen we gotta find," Cadillac went on.

"He's right, Johnny," said Goldie, recovering. "The
sandwiches are cold. There's a kitchenette in my
room; let's take them in there. I'll warm them up
while you think, honey."

"Yeah . . . okay."

"I'll get the map," said Ears. "I think I put it in the
closet."

I heard the knob turn, followed immediately by the
faint snicks of three hammers being drawn back. It
was going to be deafening, I knew that. It was also
going to be over quick. I fervently hoped the slug with
my name on it would be merciful. I never could stand
pain.

"It's right there on the bed, you jerk!" said Johnny
Cadillac. "Get it and let's go."

A moment later a door shut, a latch clicked, and
inside the closet there were five simultaneous sighs.

"They're gone," said Bass Voice.

"That was a close one," breathed Tenor.

"They took the map," grumbled the third hood.

Our fellow closeteers gathered themselves up and
ventured out into the motel room. "Let's beat it before they come back."

Once more the door clicked shut and silence fell
over the closet. "Jerry," I said after a while, "the next

time you get an idea, I want you to promise me something. *Don't tell it to me!*"

Though the method had brought about a near-disaster, and added a few gray hairs to my head, it did seem that we now knew almost as much as any of them about the final words of 'Bugs' Casino concerning what must have been part or all of the loot from the armored car job.

Back at the office, Jerry and I tried to come up with some reasonable explanation to give Dan Peavy as to how we happened to overhear the conversation. But there was nothing to tell but the truth, and I phoned him at Doc Stebbins' house and told him he'd better come down to the office. I did not have to add that it was important. That always went without saying on chess night.

Fifteen minutes later, Dan was seated comfortably behind his desk bending a malevolent eye on us. "Now lemme get this straight. You two officers of the law made an illegal entry—"

"Dan," I interrupted. "Let me tell you the whole thing, then give us the chewing out." He nodded skeptically; I took a deep breath and waded in.

When I was done—with one or two amendments from Jerry—Dan walked over to the window and stared across at the lights of the Bon Air Cafe. "That part you didn't hear, that mighta been something that pin-pointed it in Guale County, maybe even closer than that."

"That's what I figured. But from the way the rest of it sounded, he didn't tell her exactly where to look. This Ed or Eddie Allen they're supposed to see, he's got something to do with that."

Dan shook his head. "Whoever this Allen is, if he knew where the loot was hid, how come he wouldn't of got it himself?"

"The robbery was in New Jersey," said Jerry. "Casino was picked up in California. Guale County ain't exactly on the route between the two."

"Which means he musta had some pretty good reason for comin' here."

"Also," I said, "wherever it is, you have to have a boat to get there. All of 'em are getting boats, which means 'Bugs' Casino would have had to have a boat when he buried it. Now, I never heard of crooks pulling a boat around with 'em when they made their getaway, so he had to get the boat when he got here."

"Maybe from Ed Allen?" Jerry suggested.

"Mebbe," said Dan. "But there ain't no Ed Allen around here now, and far as I know, there never was. It's more likely he got a boat at one o' the fishing camps." He opened the desk drawer and produced a newspaper picture of 'Bugs' Casino. "I got this from the *Clarion*. Take it around to the fish camps and find out if anybody can remember him. 'Course, it's been a long time, but it's worth a try."

Fishing camps start the day early, so Jerry and I began making the rounds before dawn the next morning. We tried the camps on Turtle River first, without success, and then headed over to Frenchman's Creek, where we stopped at Elton Boggs' place with the intention of working west from there.

Elton was caulking one of his boats when we found him, and Jerry showed him the picture. "Now think hard, Elton. It woulda been about seven years ago, so maybe you won't be able to remember—"

"Sure I remember him," Elton said flatly, hardly glancing at the picture. "But I don't understand what . . ."

"You don't have to understand," said Jerry. "Leave that to us. Now you say you remember him. Did he rent a boat from you? And if so, did he say where he was going? And did he have a bag or something with him? A briefcase?"

I butted in. "You were about to say something, Elton. You don't understand *what?*"

"Pete," Jerry said with great patience, "I was interrogatin' the witness, if you don't mind."

"I was tryin' to tell you," said Elton, "that I don't understand why everybody's so dang interested in this fella."

Jerry's mouth dropped open. "Everybody?"

"That's right. There was two other fellas askin' about him yesterday. Had pictures of him. I got a good memory for faces, and, well as I could recollect, I rented this guy a boat and motor and some tackle. But he didn't have nothing with him. He headed right up the creek toward the highway bridge, and when he came back about an hour later he just got in his car and drove off. Didn't catch one measly fish."

From Elton's description, the two men who had come by the day before, separately, were Johnny Cadillac and Seven-Finger Norton. He also said one of them had asked about Ed Allen, but that he never knew anybody by that name. "This blackheaded fella seemed right upset when I told him that. Say, what's this all about anyhow?"

"Just a routine investigation," Jerry said pompously. "That's all, just routine."

Elton grinned and nudged me with his elbow. "Listen at him, Pete! You can sure tell old Jerry watches them detective programs on the television, can't you?"

When we had made our report to Dan Peavy, he went to the big map on the office wall, and with a pencil drew an S at the location of the fishing camp. "If he didn't have the loot with him, he mighta done this. His pals coulda been let off at the highway bridge with the money, Casino could have run up in the boat, picked 'em up, gone someplace to bury the loot, then dropped his pals off and come back to the fishin' camp by himself."

Dan looked around at us to see how the idea was received. It sounded okay to me, except I still could not imagine *why* Casino would have done it that way.

When no objections were forthcoming, Dan proceeded. "All right, so Elton says he was back in about an hour. Now I'd say top speed on those outfits he

rents is about ten miles an hour. We know he went
this direction, and if he did bury the money that
woulda taken, say, half an hour."

"I get it!" said Jerry, striding to the map. He
pointed to the marshy area that stretches all the way
over to the state highway. "It'd probably be on one of
these islands!"

Dan Peavy nodded. "There's Bishop Island, Lanier,
Palm, Hatchet, North, and Crooked Island. It must be
one o' them."

Jerry shook his head. "A dang army could dig on all
them islands from now till doomsday and never find
the stuff."

Dan stood staring at the map. "Yep. I reckon you're
right, Deputy."

For the next three weeks, the two boatloads of
hoods plied the creeks and rivers in the north part of
the county. We tried following a couple of times, but
as soon as Johnny Cadillac found that some of his fellow mobsters were tailing him, he spent considerable
time setting up decoys, digging on first one island,
then another, until he had stopped at all the islands at
least once.

Also, from the length of time involved, it was pretty
obvious that he did not know the exact location of the
loot. As for Dan Peavy, he spent more and more time
in the office, either studying the big map, or going
over the notes of Goldie's final visit with her previous
boy friend.

It was on a Thursday, with just Dan and myself in
the office. For fully thirty minutes he had been staring at the map. Finally, he turned away to ask me a
question. "This 'Bugs' Casino was librarian at the
prison, wasn't he?"

"That's right. It was something in the library that
fell on him."

"And something just mighta fell on me," Dan mumbled, heading for the door.

"Where're you going?"

"I'll tell you when I get back."

When he did get back a short time later a smug grin was plastered on his homely old kisser. "Pete, this is about as far out as anything I ever seen, but darned if it don't make a certain amount o' sense!" He looked at the clock. "Phone down to the county marina and find out if them folks have gone out today. If they ain't, tell the boy to put our boat in the water."

I made the call and found out that Cadillac and the others were taking a day off, that they had hit an oyster bank and the motor was being repaired.

"Good," said Dan. "Now, you run me down to the marina and wait there for me, just to make sure they don't come out."

"I still don't get it. What's this all about?"

He grinned. "Pete, I either know exactly where that money's at, or I'm a monkey's uncle! But I wanta take the first look by myself."

There's no point in arguing when Dan has one of his brainstorms, so I did what he told me, and watched him disappear around the bend in the river.

A little later Jerry joined me, having seen the car behind the marina. I told him exactly what had happened, which put him just as much in the dark as I was. After more than an hour had passed, the familiar green boat came racing back around the bend. Dan Peavy was grinning like a jackass eating briars when the boat came alongside the dock.

"Get a couple o' shovels and hop in, boys," he said. "I know where that loot is hid."

"You . . . *really* know?"

"Right! Now get them shovels."

Armed with the digging equipment, Dan Peavy at the wheel, and the wide river ahead, we sped north. Dan would say nothing about what he had found, or how, and when we crunched ashore at Bishop Island he got out of the boat and strode toward the three or four acres of high wooded ground on the island. Si-

lently, single file, the three of us trooped along the
bluff. About two hundred feet back from the river,
near a big liveoak that seemed to be the granddaddy
of the others on the island, Dan stopped and pointed
down at the ground. There were two sticks lying there,
crossed.

"Dig," he said.

"Dig?" we echoed.

Dan nodded, and walking over to the tree, sat down
and leaned back against the huge trunk. "Right where
I put the sticks. Dig there."

Jerry stared at him incredulously. Then, muttering
under his breath, he booted his spade down into the
earth. I followed suit, and down we went, while Dan
Peavy rolled a cigarette and had a leisurely smoke.

Down one foot. Two. Three. Jerry paused to mop
his brow. "Dan, this wouldn't be one o' your little
jokes, would it? Gettin' back at us for that motel business?"

"How far down are you?" was all he said. I told him
and he said, "Keep goin'."

The sun was bearing down and we were just beyond
the shade of the big tree. The going was hot.

But after the next spadeful of earth, Jerry stopped
mumbling and reached down to pick up something. It
was a bone. He looked it over and held it up for Dan
to see. That brought him over to the hole in a hurry.

"I kinda figured this," he said, turning the bone
this way and that. "You're nearly through, boys. Keep
diggin'."

There were plenty more bones then. A skull turned
up and I lifted it from the hole. Sometimes Indian
bones are found along the coast, but this was no Indian, not with a full set of dental plates. After a while
we had what appeared to be two complete human skeletons. On a finger bone of one was a class ring. It
read: *PS 28. Brooklyn. Good Luck, Class of 1932.*

"How the devil did you know where to find *these?*"
Jerry demanded of Dan.

"Dig a little more. I think you'll find something else."

And we did. Just below the bones we found a large suitcase, wrapped carefully in a big sheet of plastic. Nobody said a word while we hastily ripped it open. At this point, there was nothing surprising to me when it turned out to be full of money. In fact, I doubt if I would have thought it unusual if Dr. Sweitzer had hopped out and done a buck and wing.

Jerry flung his spade to the ground and put his hands on his hips. "Okay, Dan. Spill it!"

"Well," said Dan Peavy, "if there was an answer, I figured it had to be in what Casino told his girl friend before he died. I went over it until things began to add up. First, there was that Ed Allen business."

"But he never turned up!" exclaimed Jerry. "How'd that figure?"

"It ain't surprisin', him not turnin' up," Dan mused. "He's been dead better'n a hundred years."

"What?"

"We'll get back to that. Now then, the very last thing he said was what she thought was her name and his. Now stop there a minute. Just what *was* their names?"

"Bugs and Goldie?"

"Right!" said Dan with a grin. "And I figure the other thing he said, the thing you didn't hear, was that the money was on Bishop Island." He pointed up into the big tree. "The last piece o' the puzzle is right up there. Pete, shinny up there and bring it down for me."

First, I glanced at Jerry, who in turn was staring at Dan in a way that spoke volumes. His superior had obviously made a pact with the devil. Then I looked up into the tree. All I saw were limbs, leaves, and festoons of Spanish moss. But suddenly something caught my eye.

"Is that what you're talking about?" I asked Dan. He said it was, indeed, and I made my way up to it. It was one of those little plastic skulls you see dangling from rearview mirrors in cars. There was a nail holding it. I broke it loose and came down. On the way down, I realized what Dan meant when he said the thing was as far out as anything he had seen. It really was.

I tossed the little skull to Jerry, then looked at Dan. "Ed Allen . . . Edgar Allan *Poe?*"

He nodded.

"And . . . Goldie and Bugs wasn't what he was telling her, but *The Gold Bug?*

"I still don't see what's happening," Jerry grumbled.

"The Gold Bug! It's a story about a buried treasure and it was written by Edgar Allan Poe. You had to read it in high school!" I turned toward Dan. "Then *that's* where you went? The library?"

"Right. One o' the clues in the story was a place called Bishop's Castle. Well, that pretty much had to be Bishop Island, which was why he came to Guale County in the first place. The instructions are there in the story from then on, the biggest tree around, the skull nailed on a limb. You drop a weight through the eye, then make a line from the tree trunk, through the place the weight lands, and dig fifty feet out. The two skeletons? Well, they're Casino's accomplices. There were two of 'em in the story, too."

I leaned down and picked up the skull with the false teeth. "I guess it just goes to show you how reading crime stories affects some people, huh?"

Most men who might have cracked a tough case like this would have been content to have the news splashed around so they could sit back and have folks marvel at them. But Dan Peavy had a streak of civicmindedness that overshadowed his ego. Our visitors from the east were having quite an impact on Guale County's economy. There had been thousands of dollars spent for boats and equipment. Goldie's patronage of Sadie's Beauty Salon and the Bon Ton Dress Shoppe was in the nature of a bonanza for both of them. The Midway Motel and the Inn had much-needed paying guests. And there were the restaurants, gas stations, and marina bills to take into consideration. Seven-Finger Norton unexpectedy became Six-Finger Norton while cutting wood for a campfire, which gave Doc Stebbins a new patient for a while.

So Dan put the skeletons in a box, and the money in a safe deposit vault at the bank, and let the search continue. The frost was on the pumpkin when the two gangs finally gave up hope of ever finding the late 'Bugs' Casino's buried loot.

Later on, when the news broke about the recovery of the money, Dan Peavy mailed a book to Johnny Cadillac—*The Complete Works of Edgar Allan Poe.*

YELLOWBELLY

by William Brittain

The car had turned off the main highway onto the hard-packed dirt road that led through the desert only fifteen minutes ago, but already the unchanging vistas of hot sand, creosote bushes and bur sage were beginning to get to Bryce. A lizard skittered across in front of them, followed in swift pursuit by a roadrunner. If he was that lizard, Bryce thought, he'd lie down and give up. It was just too hot to run.

Outside the closed windows the alkali dust boiled up about the car, and Bryce pulled a handkerchief from his pocket and mopped his steaming face. The air-conditioner sure picked one helluva time to go on the fritz. He felt like a turkey in the oven, already basted with his own sweat. He reached toward the button on the door to roll down the window.

"Leave it closed, if you please." The words were a request which the gutturally accented voice of the man behind the wheel turned into an order.

Bryce turned to look at him. Augie still looked as if it were a spring day outside instead of the desert's blasting heat. Augie sure was a cool one. He'd set up the whole thing without one hitch, at least none so far. Even while they were in the bank he'd never lost his cool, calmly ordering the president and the loan officers to clean out the vault as if he were giving instructions to paid servants. Augie had no nerves at all.

It was Bryce whose finger had jerked convulsively against the trigger of the .45 automatic as they were leaving through the bank's side door, hitting the guard in the shoulder and slamming him to the floor. Even as they screeched off down the road and out of town, Augie had offered only a single comment.

"That was needless, Bryce. If he dies and we're caught, it's murder. But of course we will not be caught."

That was all, yet Bryce knew that Augie was upset. Augie was happy only when his plans went like clockwork.

"Augie, I—I'm sorry," Bryce said in a halting voice.

"Please, Bryce, no more exercises in self-pity. Look, already the road is beginning to rise. Another half hour and we'll be in the midst of those mountains. The police will never find us there."

"If they ever decide we came out this way, they won't have to, Augie. According to this map, the road dead-ends near an abandoned Indian village up there in the mountains. All they'll have to do is set up a blockade and then wait until we either come down or the sun cooks us dry. We only brought two water bottles with us."

"I didn't plan so perfectly just to fail now," replied Augie, polishing a tooth with the tip of a finger. "Nobody knows we're up here, and escape has been arranged by—" His head suddenly jerked about as if a string had been pulled. "Did you see that? Off on your side."

"How could I? I was talking to you."

Augie slammed the car into reverse and began backing toward the narrow bend they had just passed. Bryce closed his eyes tightly. The road was narrow, with no guardrails, and even here at the edge of the mountains he didn't like the look of the sheer drop-off on the left-hand side.

The car careened back around the bend in the road, and the brakes screeched it to a halt. "Look," Augie said.

An area of perhaps an acre had been rudely scraped out of the hillside with a bulldozer. In its center was a long dilapidated building painted bright pink, in front of which a dented gas pump stood like a drunken sentry. At the rear was a large shed, and next to it, a smaller lean-to.

At the road's edge was a large sign that looked as if it had begun life as a barn door. It was off-white, with its upper half lettered in blue:

YELLOWBELLY'S PLACE
GAS, EATS AND

Bryce and Augie could only guess as to what other delights the "and" on the sign referred.

"That has no right to be here," Augie said, pointing to the group of buildings. "It was not included in my plans."

"I guess people got the right to set up business wherever they want to. It doesn't seem like they're going to get many customers out here, though. How come you stopped, Augie?"

"Think, Bryce. This road comes to an end up there in the mountains. It will be necessary for us to wait there until approximately ten o'clock tomorrow morning before we are picked up."

"Picked up? What do you mean?"

"That is my business. But this whole plan depends on the police not knowing exactly where we are. However, we're the only travelers on this road. If anyone inside one of those buildings saw us go by, you can imagine the difficulties we'd be in between now and tomorrow, especially if the report of the robbery has been broadcast on the radio."

"Yeah, I gotcha. So what now?"

Without answering, Augie twisted the wheel and put the car in gear. It jounced over to the gas pump. Augie beeped the horn.

The door of the pink building opened. Bryce looked at the man who stepped out into the sunlight, glanced at Augie and then looked again, as if he couldn't believe what he'd seen the first time.

The man was scarcely five feet tall, with a face as seamed as a desert dry wash. A bulbous nose surmounted a fierce, flowing moustache which resembled a steer's horn. On his head was a huge sombrero with chunks torn from the brim. His flannel shirt, partially hidden by a canvas vest, covered a potbelly beneath which the waistband of his jeans sagged alarmingly. On his feet were high-heeled boots of cracked leather.

The strange little man waved an arm at them. "Howdy!" he called in a shrill, squeaky voice. "Welcome to Yellowbelly's Place. That's me, Yellowbelly Dobkins. Been workin' this desert more'n sixty years now. Like to come in and set a spell? I got some chili warmin' on the stove."

"That little wart shouldn't be hard to take," Bryce whispered to Augie out of the corner of his mouth. "I'll just—"

"Do nothing, you fool!" Augie placed a restraining hand on Bryce's arm. "Look over there."

A second man was coming outside. He appeared to be in his middle twenties, tall and muscular, with his hair cut short, military fashion. Over his clothing he wore a white apron.

The second man approached. "Name's Muggeridge," he said, without offering to shake hands. "Pete Muggeridge. Me and Yellowbelly run this place. But we ain't exactly open for business yet. Now, want to tell me what you two are doing way back here?"

"We—we are tourists," Augie began.

Bryce hoped he could make the story stick. With that accent, Augie sounded more like a Nazi general in one of the old TV movies.

"We were hoping to see the old Indian village. According to the maps, this section is uninhabited, and we expected to go right on up to it. Of course, if there is a fee . . ."

"No fee," Yellowbelly said. "You can go if you've a

mind to. But the drive's about half an hour, and that road's awful narrow, with some mean switchbacks. No guardrail neither. Quite a drop if you was to make a mistake. Besides, it's gettin' on toward evenin'. By the time you got there, you wouldn't be able to see nothin'. It'd be as black as pitch."

"If you was going to the old village, how come you stopped here?" asked Muggeridge, scowling.

"The air-conditioner in the car has broken down," continued Augie smoothly. "We were hoping you could fix it."

"Uh-huh," grunted Muggeridge skeptically.

"Tell you what," Yellowbelly cackled. "It's too hot out here to be jawin'. You two go inside. It's cooler there. Pete'll give you a bowl of chili. I'll take your car out back and have a look at it. Mebbe I can see what's wrong." He jerked a gnarled thumb in the direction of the smaller building.

"You're the mechanic?" asked Bryce, incredulous.

"Yep. Pete here, he cooks for me and does the heavy work around the place."

"If it's too hot for them, it's too hot for you," Muggeridge said. "Let's all go in and chow down."

"Nah, I don't mind the heat. Been a desert rat all my life. You folks go ahead. Just gimme the car keys."

Bryce looked on admiringly as Augie brought the key case out of his pocket and in the same motion slid the trunk key off it before handing it to Yellowbelly. It wouldn't do for him to get too close a look at the canvas sacks that were stashed next to the spare tire.

As Yellowbelly started the car with a roar and a haze of exhaust smoke, Bryce and Augie followed Muggeridge inside the diner. The long room was dim, with the only light coming in through the dust-smeared windows. It might have been a little cooler inside, but not much.

As his customers perched on stools, Pete went behind the counter and silently ladled out bowls of chili from the pot on the propane stove.

Bryce took a single spoonful and snatched at the glass of tepid water Muggeridge had put in front of him. The chili was like liquid fire scorching its way down his throat.

Augie ate his slowly and appreciatively, as if he were enjoying the choicest beluga caviar. Muggeridge waited for some reaction from him and was disappointed when there was none.

Wordlessly the two men finished their meal, and then Augie put a five-dollar bill on the counter. Muggeridge shoved it back toward him.

"Not necessary," said the cook. "We ain't open yet. And Yellowbelly's always telling me that in the desert it's best to be hospitable. Next time out, you might be the one in need of help." He turned and switched on the battery radio by the sink.

". . . From Yuma, Arizona," came the announcer's bland voice. "And now another all-time great from our collection of dinner music." The ballad was soft and low, heavy on the violins.

"Mr. Muggeridge," Augie said suddenly, "I wish to ask you a question."

"Ask away."

"Have we done something to annoy you?"

"Nope. Why?"

"You've been extraordinarily gruff with us since we arrived. I thought you were angry."

"Not angry."

"Oh? Then what?"

"It don't seem to me that anybody'd come to look at the Indian village dressed in suits the way you two are. Besides, you talk funny. I'm just trying to figure you out."

"I am Austrian, you see."

"Yeah." Muggerigde turned up the volume of the radio.

"Is that necessary?" Augie asked. "It is hard to hold a conversation with that music blaring."

"I like it."

Augie looked at Bryce and patted the jacket pocket where his gun was kept. The radio meant contact with the outside world, and they didn't like that.

Outside the window, the setting sun splattered reds and yellows across the evening sky. A door banged at the rear of the building, and Yellowbelly entered.

"Found your trouble," he said proudly, holding up something in his hand. "Busted compressor belt. I must have another one in that junk in the shop, but it'll take some lookin'. I'll need light. The lantern ought to be in here somewhere."

He began fumbling beneath the counter. On the radio, a series of staccato beeps announced the beginning of a news show. Augie looked at Bryce with a here-it-comes expression.

"Police here released the following description of the men who held up the Royson Bank, as reported earlier on this station," the newsman began. "The first, who seemed to be the leader, spoke with a pronounced accent which . . ."

The description that followed included everything but the labels on their underwear.

Muggeridge whirled about, and Yellowbelly's head appeared above the counter like a prairie dog coming out of its hole. His eyes crossed as he stared at the muzzle of Augie's gun, only inches from his face. Bryce covered the big man.

"You're them, huh?" asked Yellowbelly, getting to his feet.

"That is correct, Mr. Dobkins," Augie said. "Now hurry and get that lantern lit. It will be dark in here in a few minutes."

"But why us?" asked the old man, putting a match to the lantern's wick.

"A question in return," said Augie. "Why was it necessary for you to set yourselves up in business way out here in the middle of the desert where there are no cars?"

" 'Cuz I got a brain, that's why. Y'see, the old Indian

village up there in the mountains has just recently been declared a state landmark. In a couple of months it'll be featured in all the tourist material, and there'll be a blacktop road put in. Cars'll be flockin' here from all over the country. Now, we can't charge admission to get up there, but the people who come by will be wantin' gas and food and such."

"An intelligent decision," said Augie. "I like a man who plans ahead, Mr. Dobkins. But it was in our interest to get to the village unseen. Your being here changes all that."

"Are you—are you gonna . . ."

Augie shook his head. "I see no need for violence. We will spend the night here pleasantly, and in the morning we'll be gone. That is, unless you or Mr. Muggeridge try something foolish."

"Mister, I learned early there's some things you can't fight. So you live with them. Those who didn't find that out died early. We got no guns here, and I don't plan to go up against the man who's holdin' one."

"A wise decision," crooned Augie.

Muggeridge hurled the spoon he was holding to the floor. "Hell, Yellowbelly, I thought you had sand. You gonna let those two buffalo us? Why, if they didn't have those pistols, I'd—"

Augie leaned across the counter, brought back his hand and then slashed it forward. The barrel of his gun smashed against the side of Muggeridge's head. There was a single loud yell, and the cook collapsed to the floor, writhing in pain. His hand was pressed to his cheek, and blood was seeping from between his fingers.

"Mr. Muggeridge," Augie said calmly, as if he were scolding a small child, "I'd suggest you curb your aggressive tendencies. The next time you become belligerent, I will kill you. I mean that."

Muggeridge stared up at Yellowbelly, his eyes glittering with pain and anger. "They sure named you right," he groaned. "Yellowbelly."

Yellowbelly looked from Bryce to Augie. "That ain't so," he wheezed. "I ain't no coward. Got that name because I spent so much time crawlin' around the desert, lookin' for gold."

"Tell us about it," Augie said. "It will help to pass the time."

"Mind if I help Pete, too? That's an ugly cut he's got."

Augie shrugged and motioned Bryce to help the cook onto a stool. Yellowbelly scooped water into a pan from a barrel behind the counter and began ripping an old shirt into long strips.

"Started out in oh-nine," the old man said, at the same time daubing at the blood on Muggeridge's face. "Heard they'd made some small strikes in silver and gold around here. Figgered I'd find the mother lode. Never did. Went through many a grubstake with nothin' to show for it but a mighty thirst from the sand in my throat."

"I see." Augie seemed fascinated.

"Learned an awful lot about the desert, though, and about livin'."

"Ah. And what did you learn, Mr. Dobkins?"

"Well, for instance, some thirty years ago me and my partner, Fred Selkirk, got lost out there on the desert. Our water'd run out, too. Fred, he panicked. Took off right in the middle of the day toward where he thought the main road was. They found his bones three years later, after a windstorm blowed them to the surface again.

"Me, on the other hand, I stayed put until it was dark. Only time to travel in the desert—after dark. It's cool then. I managed to squeeze some water out of prickly pears, too. It took me near a week, but I got back safe.

"But y'know, I could of saved ol' Fred. I shouldn't have let him wander away like he done. I felt awful bad about that. So I made it a rule ever since not to run out on a partner, no matter what. That's one thing I learned from the desert."

Yellowbelly slid a stool into the lantern light and sat down on it. "Seems to me, there's things in life you can do somethin' about, and then there's other things that are gonna resist all a man can do to change them. The desert out there's like that. You live with it on its terms, or you don't live at all."

A coyote's lonely howl split the stillness. At the same time something fluttered by the window. Bryce jerked himself about.

"Pay it no mind," said Yellowbelly. "A horned owl, that's all. There's a lot of life out there on the sand—chuckwallas, pack rats, rattlesnakes and such. They learned to stay put when conditions ain't to their likin' a long time before I did."

"I like you, Mr. Dobkins," Augie said, honoring the man with a rare smile. "Your philosophy is much like mine. Change what you can, and try to anticipate the rest. I'm sure that under different circumstances we could be friends, you and I."

"Mebbe." He finished bandaging the cook's face. "You shouldn't have hit Pete like you done."

"He presented a danger to us. I merely calmed him down a bit. Removed a possible threat. I thought you, of all people, would understand."

"I s'ppose." Yellowbelly peered at Augie through squinted eyes. "You know that given the right conditions, I'd kill you for what you done to Pete, don't you?"

"Of course you would. But you're much too intelligent to risk your own life for something as ephemeral as revenge. My finger on this trigger, Mr. Dobkins, is one of those things you spoke about that resists change. Learn to live with it."

"Uh-huh. What time's the helicopter gonna come to get you?"

Bryce spun on his stool with a gasp of surprise. "Augie?"

His partner looked at him in disgust. "Mr. Dobkins is no fool, even if you are," he said. "Of course a helicopter is coming. How else would we get out of that Indian village? Would that he had been with me in the bank instead of you. Then perhaps the guard would still be in good health and the police wouldn't be pressing their search so closely."

"Not a bad plan," said Yellowbelly. "You get to the village. Nobody'd think of lookin' for you there. Now, is the whirlybird on a scheduled run, or have you got it painted to look like a police craft?"

Augie's look was akin to awe. "Amazing. The fact is, the helicopter belongs to the police. Its pilot was amenable to bribery. And we expect to be across the border into Mexico before anyone's the wiser. Oh, Mr. Dobkins, we'd have made a great pair, you and I. What a waste of talent."

"You gonna kill us? I mean, I ain't so concerned about me, but Pete's too young to—"

"No. You'll be tied securely, of course. But within a day or so the police will be up here, still searching. You'll experience some discomfort but that's not fatal."

Augie considered the lantern, glowing on the counter. "Speaking of discomfort, there's still the problem of our air-conditioner in the car. It would make things easier for us if it were repaired. Is fixing this belt a complicated thing, Mr. Dobkins?"

Yellowbelly shook his head. "Soon's I locate one out there, I can have it in place in fifteen minutes."

"Is there another lantern?"

"A flashlight. In that cupboard over the stove."

"Then suppose you get it and go finish your repairs."

Bryce stood and looked down at Augie. "You're not sending him out there alone, are you? He might—"

"He might what, Mr. Bryce? We're twenty miles from the highway, to say nothing of a city. Where's he going to go? And if he tries anything, his friend dies. He realizes this, even if you don't."

"I won't do nothin' foolish," Yellowbelly said. He took the flashlight and headed toward the rear of the building. A slamming door marked his exit.

"I think you're crazy, Augie," Bryce said. "These two must have some kind of wheels around here. That old geezer could take off, or louse up our car, or—"

"But he won't. Because that would endanger Mr. Muggeridge. Be happy we have a hostage though, for otherwise that silly little old man would do his best to kill us. And it's quite possible that he would succeed."

Half an hour later there was the sound of the hood banging shut on the car. Moments after that, Yellowbelly came inside again.

"You see." Augie smiled at Bryce. "I told you he'd be back."

"What now?" Yellowbelly asked.

"I'd suggest you make yourself comfortable. See to your friend. Get something to eat, if you like. You know better than I how long you'll have to remain tied up here, once we're gone."

Slowly the night passed. Bryce slept fitfully, his head in his arms on the counter, but Augie seemed to need no rest. His only act was to pull his jacket more tightly about his shoulders to ward off the chill evening air. The gun which he kept pointed at Yellowbelly and Muggeridge never wavered.

Then the sun rose, and the heat of the day began. Hot and sweaty, Bryce reeled into wakefulness.

"Find some rope," Augie ordered. "We should be ready to leave here shortly after nine. That will bring us to the Indian village in plenty of time for our ten o'clock appointment with the helicopter."

He turned to Yellowbelly. "Mr. Dobkins, I would like you to go out to the car and drive it around to the front of the building. You still have the keys, I believe?"

"I got 'em." Yellowbelly headed toward the door.

"Mr. Dobkins?"

"Yeah?"

"You won't try anything foolish, will you? Remember, Mr. Muggeridge remains with us."

"Never mind me," Muggeridge said, feeling at a cracked tooth with his tongue. "If you get a chance, go ahead and—"

"Leave him be," Yellowbelly said. "I'll do like you ask."

He left, and a moment later the car engine roared to life. "Smart," said Bryce. "If he'd booby-trapped it last night, he'd have been the one to get caught."

Augie accepted the compliment with a slight bow of his head.

Yellowbelly came in, wiping his face with a bandanna handkerchief. "Lucky I could fix the air-conditioner," he said, tossing the keys to Augie. "Gettin' into that thing's like crawlin' onto a hot stove."

Bryce located a coil of rope in the rear of the building. Muggeridge and Yellowbelly were forced to sit on the floor at opposite ends of the counter. Then Bryce tied each of them in turn, twining the loose ends of the rope about the bases of two stools.

Augie inspected the knots and pronounced them good. "Don't struggle," he cautioned. "The stools are bolted to the floor, and you won't be able to pull them loose. Just wait calmly until help comes."

He followed Bryce out the door and into the blasting heat of the desert day. The two men got into the car.

"Turn it on, Augie. I'm about to roast."

The engine caught, and immediately cool air began wafting out of louvered openings. Augie put the car in gear and pulled out onto the road again.

"We should make it with just a few minutes to

spare," he said. "That means there'll be less time for the police to spot this car. But don't worry if you see a single patrol helicopter overhead. That'll be our man."

The car glided along silently, moving upward on the narrow road. Still weary, Bryce put his head back, enjoying the luxury of being cool again. He turned, and through slitted eyes looked past Augie at the panoramic view spread out beyond the unprotected border of the steep road.

His brain was still mushy from lack of sleep. He felt something rub softly against his ankle. He shifted his foot, at the same time looking down to see what it was.

With a speed he didn't know he possessed, he yanked his feet up beneath him so that he was sitting cross-legged on the seat. His hands clawed at the roof of the car as he tried to pull himself up farther. He tried to scream, but nothing but a rasping whisper came from his throat.

"Augie, look! Ohmygawd!"

At the same time a new sound reverberated within the car. It was an incredibly loud rustling noise, as if someone were agitating a large glass of chipped ice with a spoon.

"Bryce, do you have to—"

Then Augie saw the thing on the floor of the passenger's side.

Six feet of diamondback rattlesnake, its body as thick as a man's arm, had glided out from beneath the seat and now lay there in lumpy coils. At one end of its body the rattles on its tail trembled faster than the eye could follow. The yellow rhombs along its scaly body seemed to pulsate, and the flat, triangular head was cocked, ready to strike. Its unblinking eyes stared fixedly at Augie's trouser leg, fluttering in the breeze from the air-conditioner, and Augie—cool, calm Augie—went mad with fright.

"Ayiiee!" His cry was one of stark terror. Instinctively he yanked at the steering wheel. At the same time his foot reached toward the brake. The shoe sole caught the corner of the pedal and slipped off, jamming the accelerator to the floor.

Nearly a thousand feet above the desert, the pilot of the helicopter was keeping the car on the narrow road below under close observation; a quick pickup at the Indian village, then a jaunt across the border into Mexico and back again, with nobody the wiser; twenty thousand bucks, just like that.

If anybody asked him why he hadn't reported in on the police frequency, all he had to do was claim malfunction. He didn't have to know anything about why radios went wrong. All he had to do was fly.

The car below wavered a little on the road. *Careful,* thought the pilot. *Just make it around that last switchback, and you're home free.* Then the car began to speed up. As it approached the curve it was doing nearly fifty. It started to turn—in the wrong direction.

The car reached the edge of the road and kept on going. For a moment it seemed suspended in space—and then it dropped.

Fifty feet below, a rock formation reached up from the desert floor. The car struck it, and almost broke in two. From there it rolled downward, and the pilot could see bits of metal spraying out from it. Then, wedging itself into a crevice, it came to rest.

A small tongue of flame lapped out from the exposed underside of the car. Then came the explosion, with flames and thick, greasy smoke billowing upward. *Nothing could survive that,* thought the pilot, *especially a hundred grand in paper money.*

Twenty big ones for himself, gone. "Aw, hell," he said.

Then he flipped the switch on the radio. "This is YP-210. You'd better send a couple patrol cars up the road to the Indian village. I think I located that car you've been looking for. Naw, there's no hurry. They ain't going anywhere."

He switched off the set and cursed his bad luck.

Then he figured that with the twenty G's nothing but ashes, he might as well rejoin the good guys.

Sergeant Barney Kowpin of the state highway patrol looked down at the incredible little man crouched in the desert dust at the edge of the road, with a brush in his hand and a can of blue paint beside him.

"Your buddy'll be all right," Kowpin said. "The doctor just wants to keep him under observation for a day or so. But there's a couple of things I still don't understand about your putting a rattler in that car last night. Weren't you running a risk that when they opened the door it'd be sitting right there on the seat, staring them in the face? Or worse yet, suppose the things had struck at you while you were bringing the car around to the front? I tell you, there's nothing that'd make me get into a car if I knew I was sharing it with a rattlesnake."

Yellowbelly shook his head. "I been prowlin' this desert long enough to know a snake ain't very lively when it gets too hot," he said. "When it's much over a hundred degrees, all he wants to do is crawl off under a rock somewhere, and the mornin' sun heated that car up fast. I figgered that thing'd stay down below the seat in the shade."

He pushed back his hat and gave the trooper a toothless grin. "Course when the air-conditioner brought the temperature down to his likin', first thing old snake wanted to do was come out to see what was goin' on." He looked up toward the mountains, where a thin shaft of smoke was still rising in the still air.

"I reckon he did just that."

"But where did you get the thing?" asked the trooper. "I can't believe you captured it with your bare hands after dark."

"Nope. Had it in a box out in the lean-to. A lot of other things out there, too. At first I was plannin' on usin' a gila monster, but I figgered the rattler'd be better. And it shouldn't be too hard to find me another snake."

"Let me get this straight," said Kowpin. "You had this snake in a box? You mean it was a pet or something?"

"Nope. Only a fool'd keep somethin' like that for a pet. I just wanted somethin' extra to charge the tourists for when they come up this way to see the Indian village."

He nodded toward the sign at the edge of the road. The new lettering sparkled in the bright sun. It now read:

YELLOWBELLY'S PLACE
GAS, EATS AND
DESERT ANIMAL ZOO

BECAUSE OF EVERYTHING

by Glenn Canary

He waited right out in the open, partly because there was no place to hide where he could still be sure of seeing Cherry when she left Herold Janssen's where she was a waitress. Mostly, though, he was just sure that it wasn't likely anyone was in Queens yet looking for him. He didn't know how long he was going to have to wait. The last he heard, she was getting off at eleven-thirty, but it was already past midnight and she hadn't come out yet. He knew she was in there because when he first got to the restaurant he looked in the window. He saw her. She was serving two men, and they were saying something that was making her laugh.

A black limousine pulled into the parking lot and stopped and he felt scared for a few seconds, but an old man and woman got out and went into the restaurant without even glancing at him. He had to smile at the state his nerves were in.

He lit a cigarette, inhaled, and tried to blow a smoke ring, but there was too much breeze.

"Damn it," he muttered absently. He looked at his watch.

A man and woman came out of the building and walked past him, laughing. He watched them. The woman wasn't pretty, but she had nice hips and legs and she walked as if she knew it. He liked that. He never was able to understand women who took being women for granted. Cherry had always been like that. She was still the best-looking woman he had ever had,

but she never thought about it. She just took everything for granted and was always surprised when some
man made a play for her. It used to annoy him that
she was that way, but he was glad of it tonight.

He wished he didn't have to do this. He didn't want
to face Cherry. But he couldn't think of anything else
to do, or anyplace to go.

Another car drove into the lot and he was watching
it when she came out. She didn't pay any attention so
she didn't notice who he was. She looked tired and
older than he remembered. She had changed into her
own clothes and she was carrying a dirty Herold Janssen's uniform rolled up and stuck under her arm. She
still had her hair long, but it was twisted into a French
knot.

He threw his cigarette away. "Cherry," he said, "I've
been waiting for you."

She stopped and looked at him slowly as if she
couldn't quite place him, and then she said, "Hello,
Ernie. What do you want?"

"I want to talk to you."

"We don't have anything to say to each other, do
we?"

"We might."

She hesitated and he smiled at her. "All right," she
said. "Let's go across the street and have a drink. That
place over there stays open late."

He smiled at her again. She didn't respond when he
took her arm, but she let him hold it. They crossed
Queens Boulevard and went into the bar.

"You still drink seven-seven?" he asked.

"Yes."

"Two," Ernie said to the bartender, who had been
listening.

She took a pack of cigarettes from the pocket in her
skirt and shook one out. Ernie lit a match for her.
"What do you want to talk about?" she said.

"Us."

"There isn't any us."

The bartender brought the drinks and set them on the bar. Ernie put down a five dollar bill, but Cherry said, "I'll pay for my own. I have money." She opened her pocketbook and took out a transparent plastic change purse that was full of silver. She counted out fifty-five cents and put it on the bar.

"What's the matter, Ernie?"

"Nothing's the matter. I just wanted to see you."

"You haven't wanted to see me since you left a year ago."

"Yes, I have."

"Why didn't you come back, then?"

"I have come back."

"You must want something."

"Maybe I just want you."

"And maybe not. You never needed me, except to support you. You always found another woman for everything else."

"Well, I need you now."

She looked up at him and started to laugh. "You're in some kind of trouble, aren't you?"

"What makes you think that?"

"I think you're scared."

"No."

"I lived with you for eight years. I never saw you like this before."

"Maybe I am in some kind of trouble."

"What?"

"What difference does it make?"

"You want me to help you, don't you?"

"I thought so. Now I don't." He started to get up.

"Wait," she said. "Tell me what's wrong."

"Nothing."

"Sit down, Ernie." She took his arm. "Tell me what's wrong. Is it the police?"

"No."

"You're sure? You haven't been writing bad checks again?"

"No," he said, "Hell, no."

"Then don't tell me," she said. "I don't care anyway."

He picked up his drink and set it down again without tasting it. "Cripes," he said. "I didn't aim to get third-degreed."

"Just tell me what kind of trouble you're in."

"Some guys are after me is all."

"You sound like a kid in grade school."

"No, really. These guys are really after me."

"Why? Money?"

"No."

"Why then?"

"Nothing," he said. "Nothing. They'd just after me."

"Did you get somebody's sister in trouble or get caught with another man's wife?"

"No. It's not woman trouble."

"What is it, then?"

"I don't know," he said. "I honest to God don't know."

"All right," she said. "If you don't want to tell me, then leave me alone."

"You're still my wife."

She looked away from him and he got up and walked out of the bar. He stopped on the sidewalk and lit a cigarette. He didn't turn around when he heard her come out, but he wanted to laugh. He knew her so well.

"Ernie," she said. "Is it bad?"

"It's bad enough to get me killed."

"Kill you?"

"Yes," he said. At least this wasn't a lie. "Kill me. You know. Like with a gun. Boom-boom."

"And it's not the police?"

"The cops don't go around shooting people."

"All right," she said. "I'll hide you. That's what you wanted, isn't it?"

"I thought maybe you'd let me stay with you for a few days."

"All right."

"I mean, I won't bother you or anything. I just need a place to stay. These guys are watching my place. I couldn't even get to my clothes. But I'll sleep on the couch or something. I won't bother you."

"Shut up, Ernie."

"I mean it. You don't have to worry."

"Just shut up, will you."

He smiled at her, but she looked away and started walking. He caught up with her and said, "You want me to carry your uniform?"

"No."

"How do you like working there?"

"It's all right."

"Is it interesting?"

She looked at him and didn't say anything, so he shut up. There wasn't anything else he could do.

The apartment was small, two rooms, and she hadn't bought anything new since he left. She went into the bedroom and threw the dirty uniform onto the bed. Then she came back out and said, "I have some beer if you want some."

"Okay."

She brought two cans of beer into the living room. "How long do you want to stay?" she asked.

"Just for a few days."

She nodded and looked down, swishing the beer around in the can. "How have you been?"

"All right."

"What are you doing now?"

"Just hacking around."

"No job?"

"No."

"Are you looking for one?"

"Was I ever?"

She laughed out loud. "Well, at least you're more honest about it now."

"I never could think of anything worth working at."

"I know you couldn't. You always did think there was an easier way to make a living, didn't you?"

"I guess so." He looked around the apartment. "If you're tired," he said. "You go on to bed."

"I'm not tired, but I want to take a shower."

"Go ahead. I won't peek at you."

"I don't care whether you do or not. We're still married. Remember?"

"I remember."

She got up and went into the bedroom. He picked up a magazine, a fashion magazine, and leafed through it slowly. He heard the shower start. It ran for a long time and then stopped.

When she came back out she was wearing a pink terrycloth bathrobe. She had unpinned her hair and brushed it out and she had washed off her makeup. She looked younger. She had nothing on under the robe and it made her body look softer.

She sat down on the couch and crossed her legs and began buffing her nails.

"You know," Ernie said, "I'm surprised you never divorced me."

"You know I don't approve of divorce," she said.

"I know, but even so."

"If you want a divorce, get one."

"Was I so bad a husband?"

"Yes."

"I guess I was."

"You wouldn't work. You wouldn't let other women alone."

"I know," he said contritely. "But that's all over."

"We're getting older."

"You're only thirty-two."

"That's older." She put down the buffer. "I wish you'd tell me why those men are after you."

"It's just a couple of guys who have decided they don't like me."

"Why?"

"I don't know why."

"I guess it doesn't matter," she said. Then she looked down and said very softly, "Why did you treat me the way you did? I always loved you."

"Look," he said, standing up. "Things happen. We do what we have to do."

"We all do what we have to do, but why did you have to be that way?"

He crossed the room and sat down on the couch beside her. He put his hand on her thigh. She didn't pay any attention and she didn't look at him.

"I never wanted to make you unhappy," he said.

"Didn't you?"

"No. It's just what I am. I can't help it."

"No, I guess you can't."

He took his hand off her leg and leaned back. "Don't you have a boy friend or anything?"

She stared at him for a few seconds and then said, "That's none of your business." She stood up. "I'm going to bed."

He sat on the couch and watched her.

She stopped at the bedroom and without turning around she said, "Come on, then."

In the morning, when he woke, she was gone. There was a DAILY NEWS on the table and a note that said she had gone out to do some shopping. He read the note and then wadded it and threw it in the wastebasket. He found a box of cereal in the cupboard and he ate some while he read the paper.

He felt good, relaxed, and he thought he could stay here a long time and be happy.

He thought about the two men who were looking for him. They wouldn't find him here because they couldn't have any idea he was married. He knew one of them was in the lobby of his building in Manhattan, but he wasn't going back there. There wasn't a damn thing worth going after. To hell with them and whatever their reason was for looking for him. He thought about that. It might be the five hundred he owed from that card game, but he couldn't be sure.

Those guys were little, they weren't likely to send around this kind of muscle, but then he didn't know. They were mad enough about the five hundred. Well, he got away by promising to come right back, and if they'd been stupid enough to let him out, they weren't smart enough to get paid.

But it made him shiver to think of what might have happened if the super in his building hadn't mentioned that they had been there looking for him.

He supposed he ought to feel guilty about using Cherry this way. But after all, she was his wife. He thought it was funny the way she took everything so seriously. She still loved him and he'd be willing to bet that she had been faithful even though he had walked out over a year ago.

He folded the paper and left it and the empty cereal bowl on the table while he went into the living room. He turned on the television set. It was the one he bought after they were married, but it still gave a good picture. He lay down on the couch and watched it.

It was after noon when he heard her open the door. He was still watching television. When she came in, she had with her the two men who were looking for him.

They closed the door. One of them said to Cherry, "Is this him?" She nodded.

Ernie sat up on the couch and looked back at them. He was surprised that he wasn't afraid.

Cherry walked across the room and looked at him. She looked as if she was going to cry. "I found them," she said. "They told me why they were looking for you."

"They'll kill me," he said.

"That's what she told us to do," one of the men said.

Ernie stared at Cherry and she said, "That's right."

"Why?"

"Because of everything."

"What are you going to get out of it?"

"Ten thousand dollars."

"What?"

"Your insurance money."

"I don't have any insurance."

"Yes, you do. That policy you took out right after we were married. You always thought it lapsed, but I kept it up. I never got anything else from you, love, protection, nothing. And I want out of this." She looked around the room.

He stood up. "All right," he said.

The two men were waiting by the door. They didn't have guns showing. They were just waiting.

"Ernie," Cherry said. "I had to do it. After everything you did to me, I had to do it. It isn't just the money. You couldn't get off free. Not after everything. I want you to understand. I couldn't just let you forget me."

He looked at her, but he didn't say anything.

One of the men said, "Come on already."

When he walked to them, they stood aside and let him go out the door first. They followed him down the hall. Cherry was standing at the door, watching, and just before they reached the stairway, she called out, "Wait." They turned and she ran toward them. She started to touch Ernie, drew back and said, "You understand, don't you, Ernie?" Cherry was still standing there when the two men took him down the stairs.

REFUGE

by Fletcher Flora

She had walked all the way to her father's house, three miles across the town, and now she had been sitting alone in her old room for more than an hour. She knew that it was more than an hour because the clock in the front hall had said almost a quarter to four when she arrived, and the five o'clock whistle had just sounded up north at the roundhouse in the railroad yards. At the first shrill blast of the whistle, she had raised her eyes and cocked her head in an attitude of listening, as if she were hearing something new and strange that only she in all the world could hear, but when the sound had diminished and died away she had lowered her eyes again and sat staring, as before, at her hands folded in her lap. In all the time she had been here, except for the brief interval when the whistle blew, she had hardly moved. She wondered if she should get up and go into the kitchen and begin preparing supper for her father, who would soon be getting home from his job in the yards. No matter. She had burned all her energy in the simple and exhausting ordeal of getting here. She had come, indeed, only because there was no place else to go. Now that she was here, there was nothing else to do.

She was an intruder in the little room that she had known so intimately for so many years. She was not welcome here. The room wanted her to leave. She could feel the pervasive hostility in the still, stale air, the corrosive bitterness of the abandoned, the sad, sour lassitude of the lost. But this was just her imagination,

of course. It was part of the encroaching terror she had
brought with her across town. The room was no different. The room was the same. There was the desk at
which she had written daily in her diary, the fanciful
log of hopeful days, and there above the desk was the
framed copy of Gauguin's Yellow Christ, which she
had admired and hung to appease some distorted hun-
ger in her heart. There on the walls was the same pale
blue paper, perhaps a little more faded and soiled,
stained at one corner of the ceiling where the probing
rain had seeped through from the attic below the low
roof. And there against the wall between the room's
two windows was the long mirror that had reflected
her imperceptible growth from day to day and year to
year, and had told her all the while that she was a
pretty girl and would be a lovely woman. She wanted
suddenly to run away from the walls and the mirror
and the Yellow Christ, but she sat and stared at her
folded hands. She wanted to scream, but she was mute.
She sat fixed and mute in the terror she had brought
with her. Having fled from the fear of death, she
wished irrationally that she could die.

She heard her father's steps on the porch outside.
She heard them in the hall, moving toward the rear of
the house. For a while, after they were gone, she continued to sit quite still on the edge of her bed, her
hands folded in her lap, and then she got up abruptly,
as though prodded by sudden compulsion, and went
out of the room and followed the footsteps into the
kitchen. Her father, his back turned to her, was standing before the open door of the refrigerator. Hearing
her behind him, he turned, holding a can of beer in
one hand, pushing the refrigerator door closed with
the other. He was a tall, lean man with stooped shoulders and long, lank hair grown shaggy over his ears
and on the back of his neck. About him, like a miasma
sensed but not seen, there was an air of stale accommo-
dation to dismal years, the atmosphere of repeated

frustrations. He peered at his daughter through the dim light of the kitchen.

"Ellen?" he said. "Is that you, Ellen?"

"You can see very well that it's me," she said.

He carried the can of beer to the kitchen table and sat down facing her. There was a metal opener on the table. He plugged the can and took a long drink of the beer.

"I was just surprised to see you here, that's all."

"Is it so surprising that I'd come to see my own father?"

"I didn't see your car outside. Where's your car?"

"I didn't drive today. I walked."

"All the way here?"

"All the way."

"You shouldn't have done that." His voice thinned, took on an angry, querulous tone. "You know I don't have a car. Now it will be late before you can get back."

"That's all right. I'm not going back."

"You'll have to call a taxi, that's what you'll have to do."

"Listen to me. I said I'm not going back."

He looked at her for a moment, now that he had listened and heard, as if he was unable to understand. He drank again from the beer can, wiping his lips afterward with the palm of his hand. "Where are you going?"

"I don't know. Somewhere. If I can't stay here, I'll go somewhere."

"You'll go back, that's where you'll go. You'll go right back where you belong."

"Do you think so? I don't."

"What's the matter with you? Are you out of your head?"

"Don't start that. I've heard enough of that."

He apparently received some kind of warning from her words, for his attitude changed suddenly. He smiled, nodding his head, but the smile was more an expression of slyness than of understanding or affection. "Well, something has upset you, that's plain. Come. Sit down and talk it over with your father. You'll feel better then. You'll see. Will you have a beer?"

Knowing him for what he was, recognizing from long experience another of his repeated efforts to deceive her, she sat down across the table from him, nevertheless, simply because she was tired and it was easier to sit than to stand. "No, thank you," she said. "I don't want a beer."

"Well, then, tell me what's wrong. You've had a foolish quarrel with Clay. Is that it?"

"Clay doesn't quarrel with me. Clay doesn't quarrel with anyone. He's far too cold and contained. He has other methods."

"Clay's rich. A successful man. They say at the yards that he's worth millions. The richest man in town. You can't expect a man like that to be like other men."

"He hates me. I can see it in his eyes. When we are alone, I can hear it in his voice."

"Oh, hell! That's crazy. He married you, didn't he? Just two years ago, he came and took you away and married you. He didn't have to do it, either. Don't try to tell me he did, because I know better. I was here. I remember how you were. No crazy talk about hate then. He could have had whatever he wanted from you, marriage or not, and he probably did."

"That's right. I sold myself. And you—because he was rich, you thought you were onto something big. You didn't care about anything else."

"You were lucky—lucky to be born with a face and body to rile a man's blood and make him lose his head. How many poor girls from this part of town get a chance to marry a rich and powerful man like Clay Moran?"

"They're the lucky ones. The girls who don't get the chance."

"What kind of curse has been placed upon me? It's almost more than a man can bear, and that's the truth. I've never had any luck with my women. All those years I had your mother on my hands, and now I've got you."

"Don't start on Mother! Don't start!"

"She was my wife, and I'll say what I please. She was crazy—so crazy I had to put her away."

"She wasn't crazy. She had a nervous breakdown. Small wonder, being married to you."

"She died in an institution. The same place you'll die if you keep on."

"It would be better than dying before my time in the house of Clay Moran."

"What's that? What did you say? You really must be crazy!"

"He wants me to die. He plans to murder me."

His mouth hung open, his mind groping in darkness behind his eyes for some sense and sanity in her words. Then, stunned by the enormity of what she had clearly said, he pushed back from the table in his chair and stood up deliberately. "I knew it. I've been fearful of it. You're crazy like your mother. Do you know what you're saying?"

"I'll say it again. He wants me to die. He murdered his first wife, and he plans to murder me."

"His first wife drowned. It was an accident. What kind of hellish trouble are you trying to breed for yourself and for me? Clay Moran is a powerful man in this town. A rich and powerful man. What do you think he's going to do if he hears his wife has been going around making such insane accusations? I won't hear anymore. I won't listen to you."

"Don't. I knew you wouldn't. I should never have come here."

"Be reasonable. Try to be sane for a minute. Has he ever *tried* to murder you?"

"Not yet. You don't know Clay. He'll only need to try once."

"Has he ever *threatened* you?"

"He looks at me. He says sly things with double meanings. It's not his way to threaten directly. He's incredibly cruel and clever."

"It's in your mind. Can't you understand that? You imagine these things."

"He plans to murder me, as he murdered his first wife, because he hates me, as he surely hated her. I think he must hate anyone who marries him. It's a kind of madness in him."

"Now look who's crazy! You ought to be right back where you came from, and that's where you're going. It's not right for you to bring this kind of trouble into my house."

He jerked his narrow shoulders, as if shaking off an intolerable burden, and started for the door. She could hear him in the hall, dialing the telephone. After a few seconds, she could hear his voice, angry and urgent.

"Is Mr. Moran at home? Let me speak with him, please. It's important."

She didn't hear anymore. She isolated herself in silence, hearing nothing, sitting still and mute. She had wasted her strength and will. Having fled this short way to no good end, she could flee no farther.

Sitting so, futile and spent, she thought of Roger. She had not thought of him for a long time, and now that she did, after all this while, she was filled with regret and fruitless pain.

She awoke with a start and was instantly attuned to the sounds of the day, perception hypersensitized by apprehension. She could hear the soft whirring sound of the electric current driving the delicate mechanism of the little ivory clock on her bedside table. She could hear the remote and measured drip of a lavatory tap in the bathroom between her room and the next. She heard the gimping footsteps of the upstairs maid, who had suffered as a child from poliomyelitis, pass by her door in the hall. She heard from a tree outside her window the clear, repeated call of a cardinal. She thought that she could hear, deep below her in the bowels of the house, the deadly, definitive closing of a door.

It was about eight o'clock. She could tell by the slant of the sun through a window in the east wall of the room. She could measure time by the distance the sunlight reached into the room. Not exactly, of course, not with the precision of the little ivory clock she could hear on her bedside table, for the distance was longer or shorter at any given time of the morning as the sun rose earlier or later in the course of the season, but she was, nevertheless, surprisingly accurate in spite of having to make minute adjustments from time to time to the inflexible schedule of the universe. It was, like her keen perception of almost indiscernible sounds, a part of her hypersensitive attunement to everything around her. Her senses had been refined and directed by persisting danger.

She turned her head and looked at the other bed, the twin of her own, across an intervening aisle. It was empty. Neatly made. Clay had not slept in it last night. It gave her an exorbitant sense of relief, the empty bed, although she had known perfectly well, before turning her head, that no one was in it. If Clay had been there, she would have been aware without looking. She would have been aware in the instant of waking even if he had lain as still as stone and made no sound whatever. She would have known through the cold, instinctive shrinkage of her flesh. She would have smelled him, the aura of him, the sickening, sweet, pervasive scent of death.

He was in the other room, beyond the bath. She could not hear him. She sensed him through her infallible senses. He was standing in utter and deliberate silence, motionless, his head canted and his eyes watching her through double walls, waiting to detect through his own acute senses the slightest movement of her body, the merest whisper of her bated breathing. Slowly she closed her eyes in an effort to preserve the secret of her wakefulness. No use. He knew her secret. He was coming. She heard him in the bathroom. She heard him crossing the room to her bed. She heard his voice.

"Good morning, Ellen," he said. "How are you feeling?"

Knowing the futility of simulation, she opened her eyes and looked at him. He was, she had to admit, very deceptive. He did not look at all like a man, a devil, who had murdered his first wife and was planning to murder his second. His body was slender and supple, just under six feet, and his expensive and impeccable clothes hung upon it with an effect of casual elegance. His smooth blond hair fitted his round skull like a pale cap. His mouth was small, the lips full, prepared to part unpredictably, at the oddest times, in an expression of silent laughter. His eyes were azure blue, brimming with a kind of candid innocence, a childlike wonder, as if he were listening always to a private voice telling an interminable fairy tale. Oh, he was deceptive, all right. He was deceptive and deadly.

"I'm feeling quite well, thank you," she said.

"Improved from last night, I hope."

"Wasn't I feeling well last night? I can't remember that I wasn't."

"Well, never mind. A good sleep will sometimes work wonders. Did you sleep well?"

"I slept quite well, thank you."

"You see? It was the work of the sedative I gave you. You were a bad girl to try to avoid taking it. They have done some remarkable things in drugs these days. It's absolutely amazing what can be done with them."

What did that mean? Why did he suddenly, when you least expected it, say such disturbing things? Why did his words, so overtly innocent, have so often under the surface a sinister second meaning?

"I don't like to take drugs," she said quietly. "I'm afraid of them."

"Well, one must be cautious with them, of course, but it's foolish to avoid them when they're needed. I was very careful not to give you too much. Did you imagine for an instant that I would be careless where you were concerned?"

There! There! Did you hear that?

"They make you vulnerable," she said.

"Vulnerable? Nonsense. Vulnerable to what?"

"Who knows? Who knows what the effects may be?"

"My dear, you sound like a Christian Scientist. Or do you? I'm afraid I don't know just what Christian Scientists believe." He revealed his small white teeth in the unpredictable expression of silent laughter. "Anyhow, I assure you that you were sleeping like a baby when I looked in on you later last night. I didn't want to risk rousing you, so I slept in the next room. Did you miss me this morning?"

There he had stood. There he had stood in the dark and dangerous hours of the night, surrounded by the silent, waiting house, watching her and watching her as she slept a drugged sleep, and death had stood at his side.

"Your bed hadn't been slept in," she said. "I saw that when I awoke."

He sat down and took one of her cold hands and held it in both of his. "Tell me, Ellen," he said, "why did you run away yesterday?"

"I didn't run away. I went to see my father."

"Your father was disturbed about you. He said you didn't want to come home again."

"My father is a foolish man. He says foolish things."

He seemed to be concerned about your mother—or about you, rather, as your mother's daughter."

"What do you know about my mother?"

"I know that she died in a mental institution. I knew it when I married you. After all, it was no secret."

"There was nothing wrong with my mother that my father didn't cause."

"It's all right, Ellen. Everything will be all right. I was just wondering about something, that's all. Would it make you feel better to see a good doctor?"

"A psychiatrist, you mean?"

"If you wish."

"I don't wish. I don't wish at all."

"It might be the best thing for you. To tell the truth, I've been concerned about you myself the past year or so. I don't know what it is, exactly. You changed somehow. You seem to be more imaginative. Confused about things."

"I'm not confused." In a moment of defiance, she looked squarely into the wonder of his childlike eyes. "I see everything quite clearly."

"Well, I only want to help if I can. You know that, my dear." He leaned forward from his position on the side of the bed and brushed his lips across her forehead. "Now I must be off to the office. You had better stay in bed and rest. Would you like me to have your breakfast brought up?"

"No. I can't just lie here. I'll go down."

"As you wish. I suggest, however, that you stay in the house today."

"Is that an order?"

He had stood up and turned away, and now he turned back, his eyebrows rising in surprise. "Certainly not. Whatever made you say such a thing?"

"I thought perhaps I was being put under a kind of house arrest to keep me from running away again."

"Run away? Nonsense. You are my wife, not my prisoner. You are free to go whenever and wherever you please."

"Thank you."

He walked to the door and turned to look back at her once more. Blue, candid eyes. The sudden unpredictable expression of silent laughter. "You are my wife, my dear. Remember that. Whatever your trouble

is, if there is trouble at all, we will work it out together, you and I. There is a cure for everything, you
know. One balm for many fevers."

He opened the door and went out, leaving his words
hanging in italics in the breathless air of the room.

*One balm for many fevers! Hadn't she heard that
before? Had she read it somewhere? It meant death.
Death was the balm. Death was the only cure for all
ills and troubles.*

Her thoughts acted on her like a catalyst. She got
out of bed immediately and started for the bathroom,
but on the way, between her bed and the bathroom
door, she caught an oblique glimpse of herself in a
full-length mirror on the wall. She halted abruptly, as
if fixed and held static in the flow of action by cata-
leptic trance, turned her head slowly and looked at her
reflection directly. Then, drawn magnetically by what
she saw, she moved toward the mirror and stood in
front of it. Slowly she turned this way and that, assuming positions as a model assumes them on display, and
her slim body in her sheer nightgown was the body of
a dryad rising in a cloud of cool blue mist from the
floor of an ancient forest.

Oh, she was lovely! She was all gold and old rose
and loveliness. She felt for her lovely body a fierce
pride and an agony of tenderness. She enclosed herself
in her own arms, in love and apprehension. It was incredible that the passing years would destroy her. It
was a monstrous and unholy crime that anyone should
want to do now what the years would surely do soon
enough.

She must delay no longer in a narcissistic spell, en-
tranced before her mirror by the vision of herself. She
had made precipitately the decision to do what must
be done, the last desperate measure she must take to
save herself, and now was the time, now if ever, to do
it.

Wrenching herself away from the mirror with a feeling of dreadful urgency, she went on, hurrying now, into the bathroom.

His name was Collins. He was an old man, tired. With a small treasure of petty graft which he had tucked away over the years, he had bought five acres in the country, and when he retired next year he was going to build a nice house on the acreage to die in. He had a coarse thatch of grizzled hair growing low on the forehead of a worn leather face. The approach of retirement had made him cautious, inclined to act slowly if he acted at all, but at least he was the chief. That, anyhow, was hopeful. It was a special concession to her, of course, because she was the wife of Clay Moran. The wife of the richest and most powerful man in town, majority stockholder of its only steel plant and chairman of the board of directors of its most prosperous bank was entitled, after all, to every courtesy and consideration. If she had been someone other than who she was, she would surely have been forced to talk with a sergeant or someone like that.

The chief looked at her blankly, wondering if his hearing, like his sight, was becoming impaired.

"I'm sorry, Mrs. Moran," he said. "I don't believe I heard you correctly. Would you mind repeating that?"

"My husband," she repeated deliberately, "intends to murder me."

Crazy, he thought. Crazy as all hell. Hadn't her mother had trouble that way? He seemed to remember that she had. Anyhow, what do you do with a crazy woman when she walks into your office and throws a bomb into your lap? Well, in the first place, you understand that the bomb is a dud. Don't get excited. In the second place, you humor her. You play along. In the third place, after you've got rid of her, you protect your pension by reporting to her husband. From there on, it's his baby, and welcome to it he is!

"That's a startling accusation, Mrs. Moran," he said. "It's true."

"It seems incredible. Your husband is a very prominent man. One of the most respected citizens of this community."

"I know how he's regarded. I'm telling you what he *is*."

"No breath of scandal has ever touched his name."

"He's very clever."

"Well, let's look at this thing objectively. Without emotion."

"It is somewhat difficult to be unemotional about your own murder."

"Yes. I understand that. Tell me exactly what makes you think your husband plans to murder you."

"The way he looks at me. The things he says to me when we're alone."

"Oh, come, Mrs. Moran. That's tenuous evidence at best."

"You don't understand my husband. You don't know him. He's clever and cruel. It gives him pleasure to taunt me. He likes to terrify me and watch me suffer."

"Has he ever threatened directly to kill you?"

"He is much too devious and subtle for that."

"Even if he had, it wouldn't necessarily mean much. I've been married for forty years, Mrs. Moran. Hard to tell how many times I've threatened to brain my wife. Maybe, sometimes, I've even felt like doing it. But I never have, and I never will."

"That's different. You are not my husband. If something isn't done to save me, he will surely murder me."

"Has he ever made any *attempt* to murder you?"

"There will be no attempts. There will only be, if he is not prevented, the accomplished murder."

"Until he makes an attempt on your life, or at least commits a chargeable offense against your person, I don't see how the police can help you."

"It will be too late for help then. His first attempt will be successful."

"Surely you understand that we can take no action

on so grave a charge as this when there is nothing to
support it but questionable interpretations of words,
gestures, looks. An assumption of intent without
proof."

"I see. I see that you won't help me."

The dull despair in her voice, hopeless submission
to what he was convinced was an imaginary danger,
pricked his leathery heart for a moment and incited a
rare flicker of genuine pity. She was hot, this one. She
had smoke and flame coming out her ears. She needed
help, all right, but not the kind of help the police
could give.

"Look at it this way, Mrs. Moran," he said. "What
reason could your husband possibly have for murder-
ing you? You are a beautiful woman. I'm sure you are
a faithful wife. You and your husband have been married for how long? Two years? The honeymoon is
hardly over yet. There is no reason at all to believe
that he has the slightest interest in another woman, is
there? I thought not. If he did have, seeing you, I'd
have to say he was nuts. You see what I mean? There's
no *motive* for him to murder you."

"He wants to murder me because he hates me."

"Oh, please. Frankly, I find that impossible to believe," he argued.

"He hates all woman. Especially the women he marries. I can't explain it. It's something inside him, something sick, insane. You'll believe me when it's too late.
He will murder me, just as he murdered his first
wife."

"What? What's that?"

"His first wife. He murdered her."

"Stop it, Mrs. Moran! His first wife drowned. It was
an accident. As an accident, it had to be investigated,
of course. Your husband and his first wife were out on
the lake west of town. They were in a motorboat, fishing. Your husband is a dedicated fisherman, as you
must know. The first Mrs. Moran was not, although
she apparently made an effort to share your husband's

enthusiasm. It was late in the evening of this particular day, almost dark. According to testimony, they were about to come back to shore. Mrs. Moran was wearing her swimming suit, and she decided, before coming back, that she would take a dip in the lake. She went over the side of the boat. It was the end of a hot day, and the water there was deep and cold. She took a cramp and drowned. She was quite a distance from the boat. Your husband tried to save her, but he couldn't reach her in time. She drowned, that's all. She just accidentally drowned."

"Are you so sure?"

"I've just told you what happened."

"Did anyone see the accident?"

"No."

"You had to depend on my husband's version?"

"There was no reason to doubt it."

"On the other hand, there was no way to verify it."

"He was heartbroken. His grief was genuine. Anyone who saw him could tell."

"Clay is very clever."

"He had no *reason* to murder her, no more to murder her than to murder you. There was absolutely no *evidence* that he murdered her. All the evidence, circumstances and possible motivation and method, all considered together, pointed clearly to an accident."

"He killed her because he hated her, as he hates me." She stood up abruptly, clutching her purse with both hands in front of her. Her face in defeat was composed, touched by sadness and despair. "You will remember what I have told you when I'm dead."

The door had hardly closed behind her before he was reaching for the telephone on his desk.

Outside, she stood with her head bowed, crushed by the monstrous burden of her hopelessness. She had neither the strength to run nor the cleverness to hide. In any event, even if she had the strength and cleverness, running and hiding were clearly impossible. Clay was too rich. His power reached too far. Wherever she

went, he would find her. Whatever she did, he would
kill her. No one would believe her. No one on earth
would help her.

Then, for the second time on the second day after
not thinking of him at all for a long while, she
thought of Roger.

She listened to the ringing of the telephone at the
other end of the line. In her ears, the ringing was con-
verted by the wire into a series of angry, waspish
sounds. She counted the sequence of sounds, one, two,
three, four, five. After the fifth, she hung up the re-
ceiver and stepped out of the telephone booth in the
drugstore where she had gone to call. She stood for a
minute outside the booth with her head bowed, as if
she was trying intensely to remember something that
she had forgotten. She had now reached, in fact, the
nadir of her despair. Roger was not at home. Even if
he had been at home, she conceded dumbly, there was
no good reason why he should want to talk with her or
see her or lift a hand to help her. Even if he were
willing to help her, which he probably would not be,
there was surely nothing that he could do. There was
nothing anyone could do, and there was nothing now
to be done. Nothing to do and nowhere to go. Nothing
and nowhere on earth.

Yet it was necessary, absolutely necessary, to go
somewhere and do something. One simply could not,
after all, stand forever motionless outside a phone
booth in a drugstore. At the rear of the store, across
from the booth, there was a lunch counter with a row
of unoccupied stools in front of it and a girl in a
starched white dress behind it. As a beginning, the
lunch counter would be a place to go, and drinking a
cup of coffee would be a thing to do. Having made
this decision, or having had it thrust upon her by circumstances, she walked across to the counter, sat down
on one of the stools and ordered the cup of coffee
from the girl in the starched white dress.

What day was it? Was it Saturday or was it Friday? She thought about this question for a moment, frowning with concentrated effort into her cup of coffee, and finally she was certain, although previously she had somehow felt that it was Saturday, that the day was in fact Friday. She had, for some reason or other, the impression that this was enormously important, making a vast difference to something significant, and she began now to try to think of whatever it was that was significant and different because it was Friday instead of Saturday. Then it came to her suddenly, accompanied by such an agony of relief and resurgent hope that she was forced to clutch her throat to choke back a burst of frantic laughter.

Friday was a school day, that was what was important, and Roger was a schoolteacher, and schoolteachers on school days are at school and not at home. If one wanted to call a schoolteacher, then, one could wait until school was out and the teacher was home, or one could, if the matter was urgent, call the office of the school and have the teacher summoned to the phone there, which was, she understood, a procedure generally frowned upon by the administration. Well, her need was urgent, desperately urgent, but she was reluctant, nevertheless, to resort to the emergency procedure of calling Roger at school. Having injured him cruelly already, she could not now impose upon him the slightest inconvenience. Besides, if she called him at school, it would be difficult for her to say what needed saying, and for him, in return, to say what she wanted to hear.

What, precisely, did she want to hear him say? What, if anything, did she want him to do? Save her from Clay, somehow give her sanctuary from death, yes, but most of all, she realized with a searing flash of insight, whatever was said and if nothing was done at all, she wanted him to recognize the truth.

He must believe, she thought. *If only he believes!*

Looking at her watch, she saw that it was almost

noon. Did school let out at three-thirty or four? She tried to remember from her own years there as a student, and she thought that it was four, but she wasn't positive, and schedules, besides, are sometimes changed. No matter. She would call Roger again at four-thirty, after he had had time to get home, and would keep calling him at intervals, if necessary, until he answered. In this resolution she was supported at last by the blind, unreasoned faith that he was her last good hope.

There at this instant was the remote, shrill sound of the noon whistle in the railroad yards. There were four hours and a half that must be spent somewhere, and it was impossible to return to the house of Clay Moran. She could never, after today, go there again. Neither could she sit indefinitely at a lunch counter in a drugstore. Wondering where to go and what to do, she remembered seeing her checkbook when digging in her purse for a dime for her coffee. She opened her purse again and looked in the checkbook and saw that her account showed a balance of slightly more than a thousand dollars. Well, there was one more place to go and one more thing to do, one place and one thing at a time and in turn.

She went to the bank and cashed a check for an even thousand dollars. After leaving the bank, she went to a restaurant and ordered lunch. She wasn't hungry and couldn't eat, but over food and coffee, growing cold, she was able to spend almost an interminable hour. Then, walking down the street from the restaurant, she saw the unlighted neon sign of a cocktail lounge and turned in, although it was something she would not ordinarily have done, and spent a second hour over two martinis, only the first of which she drank. It was then almost two o'clock. Spent piecemeal, a fragment here and a fragment there, time crept. It was an unconscionable drag from one hour to the next. She must somehow find a way to hurry the hour she wanted it to be, or to make less laggard the hours between then and now. Outside the cocktail lounge she saw, across the street and down a block, the marquee of a movie theater. She walked to the theater, hurrying as she wished time to hurry, bought a ticket and went in.

She never knew what the movie was. She did not read the posters outside, and inside she did not watch the screen. Sitting in cool and blessed darkness in the back row of seats, she closed her eyes and tried not to think, but this was impossible, she discovered, and so she began deliberately to think of the days and years before Clay, the tender time of sweet sadness when she had loved Roger and Roger had loved her. In the end she had rejected his enduring love with cruel contempt when Clay, much older and immensely richer, had seen her and wanted her. That was before the smell of death crept in. She had sold herself for wealth and security and enviable status. Good-bye, Roger. Forget me if you can. Here's stone for bread and vinegar for wine.

Time passed in darkness before the silver screen, and it was four-thirty. She read her watch and left the theater and walked down the street until she came to a sidewalk telephone booth. She deposited her dime and dialed Roger's number, but again there was no answer. She dialed three times more, waiting outside the booth for ten minutes between each attempted call, and then, on the fourth attempt, he answered at last. His voice, speaking after two years with the sound of yesterday, brought into her throat a hard knot around which she forced her response with a sensation of physical pain.

"Hello, Roger," she said. "Do you know who this is?"

There was a silence so long that she had a bad moment of incipient panic, thinking that he had simply put down the phone and walked away, but then his voice came back, interrogative and listless, as if he were asking a question with an answer he did not really wish to hear.

"Ellen? Is it Ellen?"

"I've been trying and trying to call you, Roger."

"I was at school. I just got home."

"I know. I remembered. Listen to me, Roger. I want to see you again. Will you meet me somewhere?"

"I don't think so."

"Please, Roger. Please do."

"I don't think so."

"All right, then. There's no use. No one will help me, and there's nothing I can do."

"Are you in trouble?"

"If you don't help me, I'm going to die."

"What? What did you just say?"

"Nothing. It's no use. Good-bye, Roger."

"Wait a minute. Did you say you were doing to die? Is that what you said?"

"Yes."

"How?"

"I can't tell you over the phone. What does it matter? No one else will help me, and neither will you."

"How can I help you?"

"I don't know. I only know there's no one else."

"I see. When there's no one else, ask Roger."

"I'm sorry. I didn't mean it like that."

"Never mind. Where are you?"

"Downtown. In a phone booth."

"Do you have a car?"

"Yes. It's parked in a lot."

"Come out here. I'll wait for you."

"To your apartment?"

"Yes."

"I'm not sure it would be wise. Maybe we had better meet somewhere else."

"Come or not. I'll wait here."

"You don't understand. It might be dangerous for you."

"Don't worry about me."

"All right. I'll come. Oh, Roger, it will be good to see you and talk with you again."

"Yes," he said, "it will be good."

She hung up. She had now, after a long time of terror, a blessed feeling of security and peace. Roger would believe. Roger would help. He would be her refuge and her strength, and it was time, past time, for her to go to him. First, before going, she leaned her head against the telephone in the little booth and began silently to cry.

Roger had been sitting, when the phone rang, on the edge of his bed holding a revolver. It was an old revolver that he had acquired from his father at the time of his father's death. He did not like guns, and had never fired this one, although he longed to fire it, just once, and it gave him comfort sometimes to sit and hold it. He was holding it again now, having returned after the telephone call to his place on the bed.

It had been a bad day at school. He'd had discipline problems. He was not good at discipline, and he often had problems of that kind. The principal had talked with him seriously about the problems several times. It was unlikely that he would be rehired next year, but he didn't care. It was just another failure in his life. His life was full of failures. All his days were bad.

His headache was back. It always came back. In fact, it rarely left. There was a contracting steel band around his head, slowly crushing his skull.

Ellen was coming. Coming here. She would be here soon. Ellen had been the most beautiful thing in his life, and he had loved her, but in the end she had deserted him. Another failure for him. After Ellen, his life had been sick, and all his days were bad. It had been wrong of Ellen to make him sick with hate instead of love. Now she might die. She had said so herself.

He broke the revolver in his hand. Because of a kind of inherent petty meanness in his nature which would not permit him to provide for any effort in ex-

cess of what was needed to complete it, there was only
one cartridge in the cylinder. One bullet for one
death.

Carrying the revolver over to a chest of drawers
where other cartridges were, he loaded a second chamber.

THE GHOST OF ELLIOTT REEDY

by Max Van Derveer

It was the evening of the 31st day of October, Halloween, when, round-eyed and babbling with excitement,
the group of teenagers burst into Marty's Cafe on
Main Street with the wild story of a strange glow that
supposedly was hovering over Elliott Reedy's grave.
All were amused except Jarvis Osage, who had been
caretaker at Reedy House for all of my fifty-one years
and for as long as most persons in town could remember.

"Laugh, fools!" Jarvis shouted. "But heed my
words! Elliott Reedy has come back for his missus!"

Jarvis vanished from the cafe, leaving the rest of us
briefly sombered by his peremptoriness. One of the
teens caught my arm and begged, "You're the newspa-
perman in this town, Mr. Mulden! You go look! We're
tellin' the truth! There's a glow, and it's just . . . it's
just sorta danglin' there over old man Reedy's grave.
Golly, Mr. Mulden, what if Jarvis Osage is right?
What if Elliott Reedy has come back? What if his
ghost is—"

"Son," I broke in with a smile that was purposely
condescending, "rest easy." I took two one-dollar bills
from my wallet and told Millie, the waitress, to take
orders from the kids. "I'll take a look," I told the boy,
leaving the counter stool and winking at a group of
men huddled in one of the booths. The men grinned
and said nothing.

The night was cloudy and unusually warm for the
time of year, but I could smell a change in weather

coming as I crossed the sidewalk and got into my car. I drove east slowly, under the illumination of the town's new mercury vapor street lights, toward the cemetery. I was positive youth and Halloween magic had produced hair-trigger imaginations among the teenagers, but I was curious, too. Elliott Reedy had been our town's best friend, he had died an unnatural death, and many in town still contended—a long time later now and in spite of the inquest finding of suicide— that his death had been murder at the hand of his daughter Harriet.

I shook my head in compassion. Poor Harriet.

In July of 1964, Harriet, long termed "wild," was driving the car that had crashed from a highway at a high rate of speed and had left her father crippled. Elliott had become confined to a wheelchair, Harriet had escaped permanent injury, and the town had broiled in accusation; Harriet Reedy's irresponsibility had finally produced irreparable damage. Then, two months later, came the unforgivable tragedy. Harriet had been left at Reedy House one evening to care for her father, while her mother had gone to bridge club, but Harriet had left the house to meet clandestinely Nicolas Joppa, one of the town's young marrieds. Given the opportunity, Elliott, who had difficulty but was capable of moving the wheelchair, had turned on the gas jet of an open fireplace and had died.

There were whisperings of murder the following day, sibilantly muttered suspicions that it was Harriet who had closed the house and turned on the gas jet, but at the inquest young Nicolas Joppa had finally come forward ashamedly to admit that he and Harriet had been together during the hour of death. Harriet's name was legally cleared, but Harriet became an exile. She attempted to weather the withering chastisement of the town and her mother, but had finally gone away.

The cemetery was on my left now. I slowed the car, turned from the street, coasted through the open gateway, and left the street light. The moon burst suddenly from behind the clouds and cast a sheen that glittered against the headstones as I rolled along the narrow concrete drive that bisected the cemetery. Elliott Reedy's grave was deep in the recess, but visible from the drive. I saw nothing hovering over it, not even the ground mist we sometimes get in the fall months.

The next morning Will Miller, who had been sheriff in our county for twenty-one years, entered my office at the newspaper plant and the crooked grin on his large face was enough to tell me he had heard the stories. "Well, Carter?" he said, the grin widening.

"No phenomenon," I assured him.

Frances Reedy, Elliott's widow, was next. She telephoned. "Young imaginations, Frances," I told her.

"My phone has been ringing off the wall, Carter," she complained.

"Well, you know how the town is. Have you heard from Harriet lately?"

"N-no . . . no, Carter, I haven't."

"You will one of these days."

"I truly hope so."

My phone seemed to ring constantly that day, and each caller wanted to know the same thing: had I seen the glow over Elliott Reedy's grave? Six o'clock and the locking of the plant door finally brought temporary relief. There was no phone in my car. But when I entered the bungalow where I had lived alone for eleven years, I was again summoned. I had five calls that evening before Omer Brown's excited voice filled my ear.

"Carter, you should drive out to the cemetery tonight!" he said. "It's there! I saw it! And it looks like it came right up out of Elliott's grave!"

"Now, Omer—"

"I tell you I saw it, Carter! I only made this run into town to call you! I'm going back out there!" Omer Brown, the town welder, was a stable man.

I left the bungalow and drove faster than normally. It was a few minutes past ten o'clock and the clouds had returned after a bright day. The night was black. There were several clusters of huddled spectators when I arrived at the cemetery. I left my car and immediately saw the glow. It was large, shaped like a giant teardrop, bluish in color and seemed to hang over Elliott's headstone.

Then I heard the siren. It came from the business district and was moving west. Murmurs came from the clusters of people around me. There was a shuffling of feet and bodies. The sound of a siren in our town was almost as foreign as a ghost light in the cemetery.

I drove back into the business district and followed the line of cars up the hill. My heartbeat quickened. Reedy House, stately in old-world elegance, gabled, pillared, shuttered, was on the apex of that hill. The line slowed and jerked along, and then I was in front of Reedy House. The official county sedan was parked in the driveway. I braked behind it and moved in long strides toward the light coming from the windows of the house. Our night marshal was standing lone guard duty at the front door.

"What is it, Herb?" I asked, jogging up the wide, concrete steps.

"Mrs. Reedy," he said in a voice that cracked. "She's dead."

Frances Reedy was stretched out, face down, on the floor of the library. The lower two-thirds of her body was on the carpeting, the upper third on the hearth of the fireplace. Her arms were spread wide over her head, her fingers were clawed, as if she had attempted to dig into the hearth. She was fully dressed. There was a small, maple stool turned on its side near her feet.

Will Miller was taut. "It looks as if she was standing on the stool and attempting to reach something on the mantelpiece when the stool overturned," he said grimly. "Jarvis found her just like this."

I looked at Jarvis Osage, the only other person in the room. He sat on the front edge of a wing chair, his knees spread, his elbows braced on those knees, and his weathered face buried in his big hands. He did not look up.

"Doc's on his way," Will said. "I phoned him."

Doc Blake, the town surgeon and the county medical examiner, pronounced the official death, and then told Will, "In layman's language, Sheriff, death was caused by the striking of the head on a hard surface. In this case, the hearth. I'd say death was instantaneous."

Will turned to me. "The daughter will have to be notified," he said.

"I can take care of that," I said flatly.

Jarvis Osage broke in then. His face was drawn. His eyes looked hollow as he stared at us and hissed, "I told yuh, Carter Mulden! I told yuh Mr. Elliott was comin' for his missus!"

I placed a long distance call from my bungalow to Harriet Reedy at her mountain retreat but did not get an answer. I kept repeating the call until two o'clock in the morning before giving up. I retired but my sleep was fitful. One ear was tuned for the ring of my phone, but Harriet did not return my call until almost ten o'clock in the morning. When I told her what had happened, she said she would be at my newspaper office in three hours.

She arrived in the middle of the afternoon, and sat in the chair in front of my desk, straight, tall, lightly tanned, a volatile girl of twenty-six years who, to my knowledge, had never turned to cosmetic or costume accessory to enhance a rural beauty. "Thank you for calling, Carter," she said. "No one else in this town would have." The attempt to fashion a smile did not hide the bitterness.

"I tried last night," I told her.

"I spent the night with a friend," she said. "How did it happen?"

I explained, but didn't tell her about the phenomenon at her father's grave. I saw no sense in cluttering a tragedy. When she asked if I would help her make the funeral arrangements, I agreed.

She nodded. "You are a good man, Carter Mulden. I like you. What would you think about my moving back into Reedy House now? It will be mine."

I could not hide my surprise and she almost smiled.

"I am writing a novel," she said. "That's what I've been doing all of these months. The inheritance from father, and now from mother, will give me the time."

I had no doubt it would, but I remained silent.

"Look," Harriet said with an abrupt imperious thrust of jaw, "in the beginning, mother blamed me for father's death. The two of us could not live together in the same house. But later, recently, she relented. I heard from her frequently, and in those letters she asked me to return to Reedy House. I didn't because I was happy where I was. I have the letters if you—"

"There is no doubt in my mind, my dear," I interrupted gently. "I knew your mother. But I must say you gave her very little hope. She seldom received a letter from you. She—"

"I didn't write because I didn't know what to write. I wanted to return here, but I was afraid of the town."

"And you are not now?"

"Suddenly, contradictorily, no."

"Its attitude has not changed. People here are slow to forget and forgive, Harriet. It's an inborn nature."

She looked at me briefly and then she stood. "I thought you might be the one person in town who would welcome me," she said.

"I am, but you must be aware of the bitterness, Harriet."

"I did not kill Father."

"So it was determined at the inquest, but—"

"I loved him, and I *was* with Nicolas Joppa that night," she said as if to reassure me.

I nodded. "I remember his testimony."

She met my look. "Does Nicolas still live here?"

"Yes," I said softly, "and he still is very much married."

Harriet's eyes flashed. "Good grief, Carter, you don't think I . . ." She paused, and then she drew a deep breath. "Carter, Nicolas was a mistake, and mistakes are not to be repeated. Not by me. I've changed."

I continued to hit hard. "But does the town know that?"

"So I am to be condemned without trial?"

"Unfortunately," I said, suddenly feeling a bit chagrined.

"Then I'll fight," she said firmly. "I'll kick, scratch, claw—"

She cut off the words abruptly, her cheeks pink with anger. Her eyes snapped, and she paced the confines of my small office. Suddenly she was facing me again. "I'm going up to the house now."

"Shall I phone Jarvis Osage?" I asked. "It could prevent a scene."

"He has to face me sooner or later, Carter."

"I wasn't thinking of Jarvis, my dear. I was thinking of you."

"I'll handle Jarvis," she said flatly, and left my office.

I sat for several seconds in deep thought. Jarvis Osage's faithfulness to Elliott and Frances Reedy through the years was equalled only by his intense dislike for their progeny. There could be an explosion. I used the telephone and Jarvis answered immediately at Reedy House. The explosion came after I had explained. "Damn!" he said thickly. "Why did she have to come back? She's no good! She never has been!"

"The point is, Jarvis, she is back, and she plans to remain."

"Damn!" he repeated, breaking the connection.

It became obvious that night and the next day, that any thought Harriet Reedy had entertained about my being her one friend in our town had been disintegrated by the discussion in my office. She did not call for assistance in preparing for her mother's funeral, nor did I see her. Will Miller phoned once in that interim and asked if what he had heard about Harriet planning to move back into Reedy House was true. I relayed what she had told me, and then said, "But she easily could have a change of mind after the funeral, Will."

"The town, you mean?"

"Towns can be sadistic."

Later that afternoon I walked into Marty's Cafe for a cup of coffee and found him straddling a counter stool. I expected more questions about Harriet, but he fooled me.

He said, "Understand you were one of those who saw that glow out at Elliott Reedy's grave the other night, Carter. I went out to have a look for myself last night, but I didn't see a thing. It's sure got the town talking. That, and Frances Reedy's death."

"There has to be a simple explanation, Will."

"Yeah," he agreed. "But what?"

I shrugged. "I want to say phosphorus, a coating of phosphorus on the headstone that gives off the glow at night, but how would it get there? Why hasn't it been seen before now? More logical is *ignis fatuus*."

"Huh?"

I chuckled. "Fool's fire. It's a form of light common in swampy or marshy areas. It's caused by spontaneous combustion of methyl gases sometimes given off by decaying plants and animals."

He shook his head. "I appreciate your vast knowledge, Carter, but may I point out that this isn't swamp country."

"Agreed," I said. "Okay, I was merely seeking simple explanation."

Will finished his coffee, and abruptly switched the conversation. "You got a few minutes to stop in at my office?"

"Sure. What's up?"

His eyes flicked around the cafe. "Not here," he said and I knew the first flash of misgiving. The feeling became stronger as we walked to the courthouse building, but Will did not say anything until he was seated in the ancient swivel chair behind his desk. We were alone in the office, far out of earshot of anyone.

"Carter," he said flatly, "something about the death of Frances Reedy is not right. She died, okay, just like Doc Blake told us the other night. She cracked her head against the hearth of the fireplace and the blow killed her instantly. It's official now. Doc has signed the papers. But something isn't right. I can feel it in my bones."

Will Miller was not a man to joke about anything, and I remained silent.

"You know, of course," he continued, "that I am one of those who have always thought Harriet Reedy turned on the gas that killed her father. I'll accept her being with Nicolas Joppa while Elliott died, but I thought then, and I still do, that she turned on the jet, closed up the house *and then* met Nicolas."

"She was cleared, Will," I said thickly.

"Yes," he said, nodding, "but I can have my opinion. Elliott Reedy was in a wheelchair, granted. He had mobility. But it is also a fact that mobility was limited. Elliott had difficulty moving himself about."

"But he *could* move," I said. "I saw him do it many times. Yes, he was almost totally paralyzed, but the man had determination. It was slow, it was tedious, but those paralytic hands could move the chair enough to get to the jet in the fireplace. He *did* have the ability to lean out of the chair, turn on the jet and then back away, knowing that he would not have the strength to return."

"All right, Carter, I have to accept that theory now. It's a verdict in the books. But set up a hypothetical case with Frances Reedy. Let's say that Elliott's death came about *my* way, and let's say that Frances Reedy *knew* it happened as I think it did. Let's say that was the *true* reason for Harriet leaving town. Let's say—"

"You're talking murder, Will," I broke in.

"Certainly, I'm talking murder! I'm saying that Harriet killed her father and her mother knew it! I'm saying that Frances Reedy would not jeopardize her daughter, but that the relationship between the two finally became so strained that Harriet had to kill her mother. You told me you could not find Harriet by telephone the other night. On the other hand, when you did get her, she came here in the matter of three to four hours. All right, think about this, Carter Mulden! Harriet Reedy could have slipped into town, had a fight with her mother, jerked the stool out from under her, causing her to fall, or she could have struck Frances with something, killing her, then planted the stool, and left town again! That could be the reason you couldn't reach her when you called. Harriet could have been in a car, running away from murder!"

"Absurd, Will," I said softly.

"Is it?"

It was not. And deep down inside, I was disturbed. Will's speculation—and that's all it was, speculation—harassed. I had difficulty concentrating on anything the remainder of that day, and that night I could not sleep. I rolled and tossed in my bed, and I knew that Harriet Reedy could have killed her father. I knew that she could have killed her mother. Will had made it that simple.

A few minutes after midnight I dressed and left the bungalow. Perhaps a drive would help settle my thoughts. I cruised the town slowly. The streets were quiet and empty. The night was bright and cold. Our change in weather had arrived. The first fall snap was on us, along with the brilliant moon. I drove out past the cemetery, made a U turn, and returned to the open gateway. I turned into the cemetery and coasted to the spot from where I could see Elliott Reedy's grave and the open, freshly-dug grave beside it. There was no glow over the area this night, but I saw a hunched figure dart from Elliott's headstone, and my heart lurched.

I called out. The figure continued to run, hunched and dodging between the graves.

I am not one to chase through a cemetery at midnight. I drove back into the business district, parked my car in an official county stall in the deep shadow of the courthouse building, and waited. From my vantage, I had a clear view of most of the business district. The person I wanted came along on foot in about twenty minutes. Harriet Reedy, a coat collar turned high against her head, her hands deep in pockets, walked swiftly over the deserted sidewalk. I let her get into the next block before I went after her. I eased the sedan along the curbing and called out, "I'll give you a ride home, Harriet."

She was sullen, but she seemed relieved when she was seated beside me. "It was you," she said.

"Yes."

"You frightened me," she said. "That's why I ran."

"Why were you out there?"

"I couldn't sleep, not with the funeral tomorrow. I needed a walk, and I've heard about this strange glow that has appeared over father's grave. I went to see for myself."

"Was there a glow?"

"No. You've seen it, haven't you?"

"Yes."

"Some in town say it is father returning for mother."

"Harriet, you can't believe in that nonsense."

"No, I don't believe in it, but I had to see."

"And you saw nothing."

"Carter, I'm sorry for my actions toward you the last two days. I have been wrong."

"It's all right, Harriet. I understand."

"I doubt that you do," she said. "You see, I loved father and mother deeply. And I like this town, in spite of what it is doing to me. It is the only town I've ever known. But—"

"The people may come around eventually, Harriet."

"Will they, Carter?"

Truthfully I did not think they would, but I hoped there might be forgiveness in the hearts. I hoped that eventually those hearts would accept and slowly open to the girl who needed understanding more than anything in the world. Looking at the faces surrounding us while I stood beside Harriet at the fresh grave the following afternoon, I knew my hopes were for naught. The eyes did not follow the coffin in its slow sinking into the grave. The eyes were fixed on Harriet. And that night I had to face reality. I had to warn her.

To some in our town, light in the windows of Reedy House was now sacrilegious; to others, it was an ill omen. A flame of ugliness had been rekindled. I sat on a counter stool in Marty's Cafe and listened to the cracklings as I dawdled over a cup of coffee. The town was now like a restless volcano. There was a frothing in its bowels. It seemed Harriet's name was on everyone's lips, and there was a seething undercurrent of vindictiveness that might easily erupt into a mob act.

"Carter?"

The terse summons behind me triggered instinctive caution. I turned on the stool to look at the four men crowded into the booth. They were large men, weathered autochthons who by temperament, habitat and teaching were peaceful men, born and reared in the uncluttered environment of our part of the country, but who, by these same common factors and an animal instinct to weed out and rid themselves of infringement on their peace, could be religious on Sunday and killers on Monday.

"Come here, Carter," Omer Brown, the largest of the four and a man capable of leading, said.

A silence settled on the cafe. Through it came the sounds of general shifting of bodies in the booth, the brushing of shoulder against shoulder, but the faces remained impassive. Only the eyes mirrored the decision that had been made. The eyes glittered with determination.

Omer Brown said bluntly, "There ain't a one of us who didn't owe Elliott Reedy somethin'—still would if he and his missus were alive—but you were his good friend, Carter. Before your wife passed on, you four, the Reedys and the Muldens, were like four beans in a pod. Therefore, you also know Harriet Reedy better'n anyone in town."

Omer Brown paused briefly and I stood in silent acknowledgment.

"So," he continued, "we're decided you're the one to tell Harriet Reedy we don't want her back in our town. We want her to get out. Go away. Tomorrow."

The decision was not surprising, but the enormity of their propriety, now that it was in the open, was appalling. I took a few moments to allow it to soak in before I asked, "Is it your decision to make, Omer?"

"Yes," he said flatly.

"Why?"

"Because we live here."

I inventoried the other faces in the booth. The glittering eyes were fixed on me. No one moved. I looked around the cafe. There were other groups of perturbed, and Millie, the waitress behind the counter. They were stone. They were waiting.

"You are wrong," I said finally. "All of you." But there was only silence when I walked out of the cafe.

The apex of Reedy Hill was beautifully silent and deeply shadowed in the fragile moonlight that night as I drove up on its summit. The street was deserted, and there was a tranquillity that belied the roiling within the confines of the street lamps below. It was a tranquillity that could mesmerize a man. I wallowed in it momentarily, then came alive with the appearance of the shadowed figure of a young man scurrying along the sidewalk. There was a furtiveness about him I did not like. I had not actually seen him turn onto the sidewalk, but I was sure he had come from the rolling lawn that fronted Reedy House.

I stopped the car and called out curiously, "Hello, there."

The man hunched deeper into himself and broke into a sprint, disappearing quickly down the hill.

I sat staring after Nicolas Joppa and foreboding became a weight on my shoulders.

Five gas wall lanterns illuminated the vastness of the pillared concrete porch that stretched across the entire front of the house. On other occasions, I had known warmth and comfort and serenity sitting in the light of those lamps. Not this night. There was a sudden chill in my bones. I stood at the paneled door and abruptly turned to the front lawn again. I wanted to find Nicolas Joppa out there with a ready and logical explanation. The lawn was dark and empty.

I put a thumb against the button of the door chimes and heard the faint, lyrical chiming deep inside the house. The door did not open. I thumbed the button a second time. Nothing. The foreboding became heavier. I tried the doorknob and found that it would turn. I inched the door open to the thick carpeting and soft lights of the wide hall that ran through the length of the house.

"Harriet?" My voice and her name died almost instantly, and there was only the utter silence.

I entered the house and closed the door quietly behind me, then stood with my hands on the knob and leaned my shoulder blades against the paneling. The silence pressed in on me.

"Harriet?" Nothing.

I entered the spacious, lamp-lighted front room to my left and found it neat and empty. I turned back into the hall. The door to the library opposite me was open. It was where Elliott and Frances had died. I surveyed the signs of Harriet's occupancy: the standard sized typewriter with paper rolled into the platen, the scattered sheets of typed manuscript on the desk, the ashtray heaped with cigarette butts. I went to the foot of the wide stairway and stood there staring up its length. What would I find if I went up those steps?

I started to turn back to the front door, but stopped. I went up the steps and searched the rooms of the second floor. I did not find Harriet.

Then I noticed the door at the far end of the corridor. It was wide open, inviting me as if by design, and for some reason I did not understand, the invitation chilled me. I moved toward it slowly. Light illuminated steep wooden steps that had to lead into the attic. I felt clogged with premonition, and I mounted the steps as if walking to my own doom.

Harriet Reedy, inpeccably neat even in death, dangled from the end of a new rope that had been looped over and fastened to a rafter.

Will Miller was not fooled. Nor was I. Harriet's death was murder.

"That chair being tipped on its side as if she had kicked it out from under her was amateurish," Will said. "Like the stool at her mother's feet. And that knot," he continued, "That was a true hangman's knot, Carter. Not everybody can tie 'em."

He turned on the swivel chair behind the desk in his courthouse office and stared out the window. It was the morning after Harriet's death. The day was brilliant and tranquil, but the town was on its ear. Death had jarred it out of its sense of predictability, and someone had again seen the glow over Elliot Reedy's grave the previous night. The talk about Elliott's ghost returning for his kin was gaining stature.

Out of the silence, Will said, "I checked out Harriet's story, Carter. I drove up into the mountains to the lodge where she has been living. She was telling the truth. She was sleeping with a friend the night her mother died. A girlfriend."

There was another silence. Then he had me on my ear.

"You know how to tie one of 'em, Carter?" he asked.

"What's that?" For a moment I had lost his train of thought. My mind was cluttered with the image of young Nicolas Joppa running away from Reedy House.

"A hangman's knot," he said.

"Yes," I said slowly, frowning.

"Where'd you learn?"

"I really don't remember," I said carefully. "It must have been when I was a kid, sometime, I suppose."

"Durn things," he muttered, nodding. "I never could get the hang of 'em." He blew cigar smoke at the window.

I said, "Speak your mind, Will."

His bulk turned the swivel chair slowly until he was facing me again. He drew on the cigar and studied the ash forming on the lighted end. "I guess what I'm thinking is," he said, "I don't know where to start on this thing. Harriet Reedy is dead and there's plenty of folks in town who think she shoul've been dead a long time ago. But I also gotta look at this from the standpoint of her mother being murdered, and then someone trying to put the blame on Harriet by making her look like a suicide."

"An entire town filled with potential murderers, Will?" I said. "That's fantastic."

"Not too," he said, "when you consider the mood of the town."

"But a moment ago you were including me."

He sat silent for a long time, his large face wrinkled. Then he shifted uncomfortably in the chair. "You had a son once, Carter," he said carefully, "an only child. The boy drowned in his ninth year when he fell from a raft into the river. I remember that day. He had been forbidden to go on that raft, but a girl named Harriet Reedy took him on it anyway."

"I did not kill her, Will."

The silence that settled around us this time became mountainous. Will stared. I stared. It was as if each was attempting to see behind the eyes of the other. Will finally broke. He sat back in his chair with a heavy sigh and said, "I got you riled, didn't I?" He almost grinned.

"You did."

"But you realize what I'm up against."

"Who has purchased a length of rope in the last couple of weeks? How many business places in town offer rope for sale? Four, perhaps five?"

Will reached for the telephone on his desk. "Yeah, the rope was new," he said softly. "That's darn good thinking, Carter."

The only trouble was, the last rope sale anyone could remember making had occurred almost a month earlier, and it had been a coil of one hundred and fifty feet to a farmer who resided in the next county.

Was this the moment for me to speak Nicolas Joppa's name?

The phone on Will's desk jangled and he swept it against his ear. Listening to his grunted conversation, I knew it was the county medical examiner on the other end of the line, making his report.

When Will put the phone together, he said, "Doc says there's a bruised spot under Harriet Reedy's jaw. He figures she was struck, then strung up."

Carefully I asked, "Nicolas Joppa served a hitch in the Navy, didn't he?"

"Yep." He frowned.

"And sailors know the various knots, learn how to tie—"

"Yep."

"I saw him at Reedy House last night."

Nicolas was frightened and indignant when we accosted him in the D&H Hardware where he had been a clerk since graduating from high school in 1959. It was the noon hour, twelve to one, there were no customers, and Nicolas was the only employee in the store, as he was every day from twelve to one. He attempted to lie. "You didn't see me, Carter Mulden!" he said with color flooding his face. "What are you tryin' to do to me?"

"You want me to ask your wife if you were home all evening?" Will asked him, nonplussed.

"You leave Cassandra out of this, hear?" the young man rasped.

Nicolas Joppa was rigid with rage. "It's my word against his!" he shrilled at Will, while stabbing a finger at me.

"I saw you, Nicolas," I said flatly. "You were coming away from the house."

"I was walking *past* the house!" he yelled.

And then his jaws snapped shut, and we were standing in the ringing silence of the store as Nicolas struggled in the consternation of being caught up in the prevarication.

"All right," he said sullenly. "I heard Harriet had come back to stay. I didn't know why. I thought . . ." He hesitated, sought words, then continued belligerently, "I thought maybe she came back to make trouble for me."

"What kind of trouble?" Will asked gently.

"Well . . . I thought maybe she was gonna try to cause trouble between me'n Cass."

"Why would Harriet Reedy want to do that?"

"I . . . dunno. Maybe she was holdin' a grudge or somethin'. You know, maybe she was still thinkin' about how I had to tell them at that inquest how she and I were . . . were out together the night . . . the night her daddy—"

"Nicolas, your testimony at the inquest was on *behalf* of Harriet," I put in. "Without it, she might have been charged with murder."

"Yeah." He shuffled nervously.

"If anything, Harriet was grateful. After all, you could have denied being with her that night."

The shuffling increased as he struggled in the mire

of a guilty conscience. "Well," he said defensively, "Cass forgave me once. I don't figure she would again."

"So you went up to Reedy House," Will prodded.

"I saw the lights," Nicolas mumbled. Then he looked Will straight in the eye. "But I didn't talk to her," he said defiantly. "I went up, okay, but I couldn't make myself go to the door. I was . . ." He shot a glance at me. "I was standin' out front, tryin' to make myself go on, when I saw the headlights comin' up the hill. They scared me, and then when I recognized Carter's car, I ran."

"Did you see anyone else around there?" Will asked.

"N-no." Nicolas shook his head doggedly. "Nobody but Carter in his car."

Will looked at me. His brows were lifted. He remained silent, but I knew he was debating. Nicolas Joppa could be lying. He'd had the opportunity to kill Harriet. He could have taken a length of rope from the hardware store without anyone knowing. He could have gone up to Reedy House, accosted Harriet, struck her and fashioned the clumsy attempt at making her death appear to be suicide. That attempt was just amateurish enough to be Nicolas Joppa's doing. On the other hand, it was difficult for me to accept a guilty conscience over a brief infidelity as motive for murder. And there was the death of Frances Reedy. Had it been murder or accident?

I walked out of the store. Will remained inside a few seconds before joining me in the warm sun. He lit a cigar, listened to my reasoning and nodded thoughtfully.

We walked to Marty's Cafe where, over hot beef sandwiches and milk, he surprised me. He said, "Actually, Cass Joppa might have more reason than Nicolas to want Harriet out of the way."

I pondered it. "Fear of losing her husband?"

"Well, he showed an interest in Harriet once. And with her returning . . ."

Will became silent, and I attacked my sandwich. Then I bobbed my head at the wide back of a man straddling a counter stool. "He also had an interest, remember?"

Will frowned at Philip Gunzan, a bachelor of midthirty years, manager of the lumber yard and Cassandra Joppa's brother.

"At the inquest?" I prodded.

Will's frown deepened. "I remember Pip was angry," he said in a guarded tone.

"And after?"

Will was thoroughly puzzled.

"Pip Gunzan threatened Harriet," I said, refreshing his memory. "Told her to leave town."

"Yeah," Will said thoughtfully. "But I always figured that was his anger talking."

"I'm sure it was," I agreed. "But the threat was made. And he *did*—still does, I imagine—blame Harriet for that business with Nicolas. Pip always felt she enticed his brother-in-law into their rendezvous."

"So do a lot of other folks. And plenty of those folks made threats, too," Will hedged.

"But Pip *is* Cassandra Joppa's brother, and we all know how protective he can be when it comes to Cass," I pressed on.

Will sat back in the booth and relighted his cigar. "Carter, if I didn't know you, I'd think you were trying to pin Pip Gunzan to a wall."

I shook him off in exasperation, but I couldn't resist the dig, "Haven't you grabbed at a few straws today, too?"

He had every reason to be irked, I suppose, but he grinned wryly, then left the booth. "Come on, Sherlock, let's go over to my office."

Pip Gunzan turned on the stool with a one-sided grin for us, but his eyes were hard as he said, "Sheriff, my ears are burning. I didn't get all of that conversation but I got enough to get the gist."

Will stared at him, and I knew he was organizing

his thoughts. Then he said, "All right, you overheard, Pip, so maybe we can make all of this a bit easier for both of us. Were you home last night?"

"I was not," Pip said, clipping the words. "I was fishing at the river."

"Anyone see you there?"

"Four or five."

"They know you?"

"Who in this town doesn't?"

"What time did you go fishing?"

" 'Bout seven o'clock."

"So you're getting excited about nothin', aren't you, Pip? You couldn't very well have killed Harriet Reedy."

"Which doesn't mean I won't pat the guy, or the ghost, who did on his back," Pip Gunzan said icily.

Will rocked the big man back on his heels then. He said, "You might start with your brother-in-law, fella."

Pip wasn't ready for that one, and we left him sitting there on the stool with his mouth open and his eyes changing expression. Outside, Will clamped down hard on his cigar. His greeting to Omer Brown, who was turning into the cafe, was a grunt. Omer shot me a significant look. "Looks like somebody beat you up the hill last night, huh, Carter?"

Before I could retort, he was inside Marty's, and the door had closed behind him. I went after Will who already was stomping across the street.

He was angry when I caught up with him. "Do you suppose, Carter," he growled, "you could be right about Pip? The guy is big enough, strong enough. And he sells rope at the lumber yard, doesn't he?"

"Let's think about it," I said.

But there was no time for thinking. Jarvis Osage was waiting for us in Will's office. He was sitting back in Will's chair and staring out the window, a thin, gnarled celibate of sixty-odd years, with a full head of bushy white hair and bright eyes that would never tell anyone what was going on behind them. He turned at our entry, but he did not leave the chair. "Saw you two comin' over from the cafe," he said grimly, "so I waited. What am I to do about Reedy House now? Close it up?"

"Leave it as it is for a while, Jarvis," Will said. He looked at me. "Incidentally, what does happen to that place now? I don't know of any blood relatives."

"Neither Elliott nor Frances had brothers or sisters," I said. "I imagine everything went to Harriet. It's a question now, I suppose, of whether or not she ever bothered at any time to have a will drawn."

Jarvis Osage sniffed loudly. "Not her," he said disdainfully. "She wouldn't have sense enough to think about anybody but herself."

I had to defend her. "Did you ever allow yourself the opportunity to get to know her, Jarvis?"

His eyes narrowed and his lips became a thin line. "She was a blight on the mister and missus from the second she was born," he said viciously.

"Funny, I knew Elliott and Frances all of my life, and I never—"

"Not like I knew 'em!" Jarvis Osage interrupted stoutly. "They was decent folks! They treated a man right! They—"

"And Harriet didn't treat you right?"

He reverted. "She shouldn't have been," he said sullenly. "That's all."

"Because she was independent?"

"Huh?" Jarvis Osage squirmed in puzzlement. "I dunno what you mean by that, Mr. Mulden, but—"

"I mean she thought and acted on her own."

"Yeah, she sure did that, all right."

"She wasn't always right, but she wasn't always wrong either."

"It was wrong when she was born to the mister and missus," Jarvis said preemptorily. "Look what she done to them!"

"Jarvis, Will and I want to know one thing. Did you kill her?"

He was out of the chair. His eyes were bright slits and his face was livid. "Mr. Mulden," he said in an angrily controlled voice, "all of a sudden, I don't like you."

"Did you kill her?"

He came around the desk and walked to the door. Suddenly he stopped and looked at us over his shoulder. "Not me, Mr. Mulden," he said. "It was the mister's ghost. The mister had a right to kill her any way he could."

And then Jarvis was gone.

We stood for several seconds in silence before Will finally went around his desk and sat down with a heavy sigh. "Everybody sure is on edge today," he commented.

"Was I too far out?" I asked, still ruffled.

He puffed on the cigar. "No," he said slowly. "I've been thinking about Jarvis too."

"I'm not sure he is capable of murder, but . . ."

I didn't finish it. I sat in the chair in front of the desk, and Will grunted, "I can say the same thing about every living soul I know, Carter."

"I think Jarvis at one time expected to inherit Reedy House," I said, more to myself in thought than to Will Miller.

"About that place, Carter," he said, "what does happen to it? The furniture? Harriet's things?"

"I don't know," I said truthfully.

"Do you suppose Harriet might have left a will?"

I shrugged.

"I'm interested," he said thoughtfully.

"We can look. We can begin at the house. There's a wall safe."

"And just how do we get into it?"

I pondered. No one I knew would have the combination to the safe. Of course, Elliot, Frances, or Harriet might have left it noted somewhere, but we could look for days and not find the secreted numbers.

"There's Omer Brown," I said finally.

"You mean cut into the safe." Will considered it for a moment before he said, "I guess it might be important. Let's go over to Marty's and get Omer."

I begged off. "I want to stop at the newspaper. Got a couple of things that need checking. I'll meet you at Reedy House in twenty minutes."

It was one-thirty in the afternoon when I again walked out of the newspaper office and drove up the hill. The car reflected in my rear view mirror was not the sheriff's sedan, and I frowned at the reflection until I recognized Nicolas Joppa. He braked behind me in the drive at Reedy House and left his car quickly. He was waiting on the grass for me when I left my car. He looked angry, and I hesitated.

"Come on, come on," he said truculently. "This ain't gonna take long, Carter Mulden. How come you were makin' me out a murderer to Will Miller?"

I took a second to glance around. Nicolas and I seemed quite alone in the sparkling sunlight.

"Are you a murderer?" I asked him carefully.

He launched a looping swing with his right arm. At fifty-one, I didn't have the agility of my youth, but he was so wide open in his attack it was very little trouble to step inside his blow. I rammed both palms into his middle and pushed him away. He yelped, his fist grazed my shoulder and then he was stumbling backward, off-balance. He sat down hard on the grass. An oath erupted from him, he scrambled around until he was on his hands and knees, and I prepared for his second onslaught. Will Miller stopped it. He rocked the official sedan to a halt behind Nicolas Joppa's car, and he was with us in an instant.

"What's going on here?" he snapped.

I told him. I expected another eruption from Nicolas but it did not come.

"You wanna explain, Nicolas?" Will asked.

"No," the young man said sullenly.

Will paused, then said firmly, "You're gonna have to

come with me, Nicolas. I don't like the way things are adding up."

"You mean you're arrestin' me?" Nicolas bleated.

"I'm not gonna put you on the book till I talk to you," Will said. "But you gotta go to the office with me."

"Do you want me, too, Will?" I asked.

"No. You and Omer see what you can do with that safe. I'll be back."

"Do you think Nicolas killed her?" Omer Brown asked, after we had watched Will and Nicolas drive away.

"You never know about people, Omer," I said as we went up to the house.

I used the front door key Will had left with me, and five minutes later Omer Brown had a portable cutting rig set up in the library.

Suddenly we were interrupted. Jarvis Osage appeared in the doorway. He looked angry. "What you two think you're doin'?" he snapped.

I told him.

He colored with rage and came across the room. "You ain't gonna tear into nothin'. Ain't you got no respect for this place or the dead?"

He went to the safe and dialed the combination. When he swung the door open, I stared at him.

"The mister once gave me the combination, in case of emergency," he said sourly.

I searched the safe then and found nothing but a few papers that had no bearing on murder.

Will Miller returned to the house and was disappointed when I told him what I had found. Then he said, "Amos Rand. Amos has been the Reedy family attorney for as long as I can remember. We should have gone to him in the first place."

Amos was a wealth of information. After the accident, Elliott had put everything he owned in his wife's name, and then Frances Reedy, in the event of her death before Elliott or Harriet, had drawn a will, leaving seventy-five per cent of the estate to Elliott and twenty-five per cent to Harriet. Then had come Elliott's death and Frances Reedy's bitterness. She had changed the will, leaving the entire estate to Jarvis Osage. Time, however, had healed the wound, and on the morning of her death she'd had a third will drawn, leaving $2,500 to Jarvis and the remainder to her daughter. Amos said he had no knowledge of a will drawn by Harriet.

"Where are those wills, Amos?" I asked.

"I have copies filed here and, of course, Frances had copies."

"She kept them at Reedy House?"

"She could have," he said, "or in a bank safety deposit box. I don't know."

"If she kept them at the house, they probably would have been in the wall safe, right?"

"I would think so," he said.

"I didn't find them."

He seemed genuinely surprised. "You have been in the safe?"

Will explained quickly, but Amos Rand did not like the entry. "I assume," he said a bit stiffly, "you found the money."

"What money?" I asked, snapping erect.

"Frances kept a considerable amount of cash in that safe," the attorney said. "Too much. Normally, it was around $10,000."

"Will?" I said, arching a brow at him as my thoughts churned.

"With you, Carter," he said, leaving his chair. He remained silent until we were outside and seated in the county car. Then he said, "Ten thousand dollars. What are you thinking, Carter?"

"We have to make two assumptions. One, Jarvis Osage knew about the wills and changes and, two, he knew about the money in the safe."

"Go on."

"Frances died the day she had a third will drawn. Jarvis, who once had been going to inherit a fortune, now was to be given a pittance in comparison. He became angry, struck Frances, or jerked the stool from under her, causing her death. He made that death look like an accident, and took the money from the safe. Remember, he knew the combination, and at that moment ten thousand dollars was much more than he was to inherit. Then Harriet returned to Reedy House and—here we have to assume again—Harriet knew her mother kept a large sum of money in the house, did not find it, and questioned Jarvis. Jarvis became frightened, killed her, and attempted to make her death look like suicide."

We found Jarvis at Reedy House. He was sullen, and when he reluctantly opened the front door to us, it was as if we were invading a sanctuary.

"We came for the money, Jarvis," Will said bluntly.

He jerked and his eyes became glittering slits. He almost crouched.

"Where is it?" Will demanded.

Jarvis broke. He attempted to bolt, but Will Miller was quick. He caught Jarvis' right arm and spun him into a wall. I moved in on the other side and captured a wrist. Jarvis was like an animal. He snarled and struggled savagely. Then, abruptly, he was finished. All of the tension and fight left him, and he sagged. He confirmed my thinking about the deaths of Frances and Harriet Reedy in broken words that were almost a babble, before surprising us. He said he had turned on the gas that had killed Elliott Reedy. He had watched Harriet leave the house that night. Elliott was suffering, and it was not right the man should suffer. He had put Elliott Reedy out of his misery.

We took Jarvis Osage to a cell in the county jail and an angry Nicolas Joppa was allowed to go home. Now there was only Harriet's funeral ahead. I had assumed the responsibility for that funeral, and that night, while settling details with the funeral director, I received the call from Will.

"Elliott Reedy's ghost is back," he said wearily. "The glow. I'm going out to the cemetery and settle this thing. Do you want to come along?"

He picked me up in the county car. It was a raw, misty night, almost foggy, and the reflection of the car headlights bounced high against the mist as we drove to the cemetery. There was a single cluster of citizens huddled a safe distance from the glow.

Will and I walked around and around Elliott's grave, studying the glow in silence. Occasionally the glow seemed to flicker. Then I stood back and inventoried the other headmarkers in the area as I recalled the other nights the glow had been visible.

"If there is moonlight . . ." I murmured.

"What?" Will asked sharply.

"The glow appears only on cloudy nights," I said.

"Are you sure?"

"Almost. At least, I remember that it was cloudy when the kids were out here that first night, but the moon had broken through the clouds by the time I arrived."

"You could have something, Carter," Will admitted, nodding.

"Then it has to be a reflection," I said. "A reflection that becomes obliterated when there is light."

"Okay, I'll buy," Will said.

"Get a blanket from your car."

We tried several headstones before we found the right one. It was several yards to the right of Elliott's grave, but by placing the blanket over the stone we eliminated the glow.

"I don't understand," Will said, shaking his head.

"I think I do," I said, grinning suddenly. "Our new street lights. They are mercury vapor, and somehow they cause the reflection on cloudy nights. Elliott's ghost is no more than a reflection."

I removed the blanket from the headstone and the glow reappeared.

A LONG TRIP FOR JENNY

by F. J. Smith

When Jenny came back from the corner newsstand with the *Sunday Times-Picayune* under her arm she found Rocky standing at the window gazing down into the grimy alley where a stray mongrel was doing his best to remove the lid from a trash can. Rocky waited until the dog finally gave up in despair and slunk off with its ears drawn back and face almost touching the ground, then he shook his head and turned away.

Jenny removed her sunglasses and dropped into a chair. Her rich chestnut hair was pulled back and she had not put on makeup. The strain of sleeplessness showed on her face, for she had tossed and turned most of the night in the airless little apartment. She felt irritable, and the four block walk to the newsstand and back in the steaming New Orleans heat had done nothing to improve her disposition.

"What kept you so long?" Rocky asked.

"It's hot out, in case you don't know it," she replied. "I took my time. Do you have any objections?"

"Kind of grumpy this morning, aren't you?"

"I'm beat. You'd be, too, if you'd slept as little as I did." She looked at him imploringly. "Rocky, when are we going to get out of this dump?"

Rocky ran fingers across his chin and along the side of his face. He hadn't been out of the apartment for a single minute in the past five days, nor had he shaved during all that time. The coarse black stubble that covered his face gave him a dirty and repulsive appearance.

"Maybe in about five days," he said. "Maybe a week. We'll see how it goes."

Jenny sighed. "If we don't get out of here soon I'll be climbing the walls."

"You think I'm having a vacation?" He gave her a pat on the cheek and added with a smile, "Chin up, baby." Against the black whiskers his teeth looked very white. For a moment he seemed about to kiss her. Jenny hoped he wouldn't. The thought of those stiff black bristles touching her skin gave her a chill. Rocky had always been clean-shaven but now he looked like a bum, a stranger whom she could not quite recognize.

"We'll have a ball when we get to Miami," she heard him say. "We'll really go out on the town."

"Sometimes I wonder if we ever will get there," she said. "Right now Miami seems as remote as the moon."

"We'll get there, all right. Don't you worry that pretty little head of yours about that." He felt his chin again. "How do you think I'll look with a beard?"

"I haven't any idea. Right now you look like—"

"I know. Like a bum. Wait'll I trim it, though. I'll have one of those goatees and a moustache that curls on the ends. With a pair of glasses and that dark blue suit of mine, they'll think I'm a college professor strictly from squaresville, not worth a second glance."

Looking at him, she could not see how anybody would possibly mistake him for a college professor. She said nothing.

"I'll walk out of here carrying that briefcase, with the money and gun, right past every cop in town, and not one of them will suspect who I am. Won't that be a laugh?"

"It will be a scream."

"Chin up," he said, patting her again. Then, picking up the paper, he walked to the divan and stretched himself out. He looked over the front page first and then went to the comics while Jenny sat, staring ahead in stony silence.

She had known all along that Rocky wasn't too strong in the brain department, but until five days ago, she had never fully realized what a bumbling idiot he really was. There had been no need to fire the gun. She had been parked at the curb, seated behind the wheel of a stolen car with the engine running, in a position to observe almost everything that had happened. Just as he was leaving the loan company one of the clerks had panicked and let out a scream. Instead of making a dash for the car, Rocky had swung around and fired one shot. The tragic part of it was, not only had the shot been fatal, but the victim had happened to be the niece of an important politician. Now every policeman and plainclothesman in the city was doing his utmost to find the killer.

It was little consolation to Jenny to know that she was free to come and go as she pleased, for on the day of the robbery she had been dressed like a man, wearing one of Rocky's sport shirts and one of his snap-brim hats pulled down over his face with her hair drawn up underneath it. They were looking for two men, not a man and a woman.

She was still pondering these things when Rocky's voice broke in upon her thoughts. He had been turning the pages of the society section when something caught his eye.

"Listen to this," he said. "Mr. and Mrs. George Devereux were hosts at a cocktail party Saturday given at their Lake Shore home. Among those present were . . . And it goes on to tell how she's taking a trip out to the Coast to visit her old man who's a big stockbroker out there."

"Isn't that nice," Jenny said dryly. "I had no idea you were so concerned with social events."

"I'm not. I thought you might be." He folded the paper and tossed it over to her. "Have a look at the picture."

Jenny unfolded the paper and glanced down in a detached way. She found the picture near the bottom, and a look of surprise came to her face. It was the picture of a young man and a young woman, both of them poised and self-satisfied with the assurance that comes of wealth. It was not the man who held her attention, but the woman. So closely did she resemble Jenny that she might have been looking at a picture of herself.

Rocky was watching her slyly, with a smile plastered on his mouth. "I didn't know you had a twin sister in New Orleans," he said.

Jenny paid no attention to him. With a shrug of her shoulders she threw the paper aside.

She closed her eyes, and her thoughts drifted to a home on the Lake Shore and the couple named Devereux. The name had a magical ring to it and she wondered about this woman, so much like herself in some ways and yet so remote, existing in an incomprehensible world of luxury, doted upon and pampered. She tried hard to visualize this world as she thought it might be, and then with a wistful sigh she opened her eyes, exchanging the vision for her own sordid surroundings. Was there nothing more to life than moving from city to city, she wondered, pulling small heists, living high-on-the-hog one day and in flea bags the next?

When they got to Miami it would be the horse races. Rocky was a confirmed racetrack tout with a line of hot tips and a phenomenal record of failure. The money would soon be blown, and the cycle would begin all over again—the endless treadmill that led to nowhere.

Suddenly it seemed incredible to her that she had ever loved Rocky, or even thought she had loved him.

"How about getting us a beer?" Rocky said.

Jenny got up and walked into the kitchen, took one can of beer from the refrigerator and brought it back to the parlor-bedroom.

Rocky asked, "How come you're not having one?"

"You know I don't care for beer."

She watched him snap off the tab and gulp down a swallow. Then she said, "Rocky, twelve thousand dollars is a lot of money, isn't it?"

"It's not what you'd call small change."

"Divided in half it's six thousand dollars each."

He eyed her suspiciously. "Who said anything about dividing it in half?"

"Rocky, I've had it. I want out. I want my half."

"Try and get it," he challenged.

"I want it, Rocky," she said in a calm voice. "I've earned it. I'm entitled to it. If it weren't for me you'd be in jail right this minute with a murder charge facing you."

"How do you figure that?"

"You wouldn't have any food or beer or cigarettes. You wouldn't have anything. You'd have to leave this apartment to get them, or else starve, and when you did you'd be picked up in five minutes and hauled into jail. In case your memory is short," she went on, "I'm the one who rented this apartment. As far as you're concerned that slattern of a landlady doesn't even know you exist."

"You're getting all hepped up about nothing. I told you before, we'll be out of here in about five days. Just as soon—"

"I don't intend to wait that long. I'm leaving now. Today."

"Walking out on me. Just like that," he said, and snapped his fingers.

"Just like that. I told you I've had it." She paused. "Listen to me, Rocky. The rent is paid up for a whole week in advance. Before I leave I'll see to it that the place is stocked with food, cigarettes and beer, and anything else you need, enough to last you a whole week. By that time your beard should be grown in and you can walk out of here then without having to worry."

"No dice! Try touching that briefcase and you'll

find yourself with a handful of broken fingers." Suddenly his face softened and a smile came to his lips. He caught hold of her hand and pulled her down beside him.

She sat limply, offering no resistance, and Rocky put his arm around her shoulders.

"You're all on edge," he said. "You're a bundle of nerves. You didn't get any sleep. This place is a dump, not even fit for human beings. You think I don't understand? I've got to sit here all day, looking at four walls. At least you can go outside, get some air. I can't even stick my head out the window in case someone will see me and report it." His arm tightened around her and he leaned forward and looked into her face. "Look at it this way; a week from now we'll be in Miami, loafing on the beach and living in some swanky hotel, with twelve thousand dollars in our jeans. We might even get married and make everything legal. How would you like that?"

She didn't answer. She could see the futility of trying to reason with him any further, and Rocky did have a temper, a nasty one. Well, at least she had tried, and now that she had failed she would have to devise another way to elude him.

"Now, how about getting me another beer," he said. "I'm empty. Get one for yourself, too. It will do you good."

She took just one and gave it to Rocky. There were only two left and by noon he had them finished. He could drink beer all day with practically no ill effects. By the same token, whiskey hit him hard and he usually avoided it.

Early that afternoon Jenny went out for more beer. She came back with six cold cans in a paper bag and a bottle of whiskey. When Rocky saw the whiskey a scowl came to his face.

"Who's that for?"

"It's for me."

"You plan on killing a whole fifth of whiskey?"

"I might, Rocky. I just might."

They whiled away most of the afternoon the way they usually did, playing gin rummy. Rocky drank his beer and Jenny her whiskey. Each time she went into the kitchen to refill her glass she measured out what looked like a full shot and then poured most of it down the sink, mixing what was left with water. The drink she brought back with her was colored enough to make it look authentic although it contained no more than a tablespoonful of whiskey.

When Rocky ran out of beer and told her to get him some more she gave him a dazed look and said in a slurry voice, "Rocky, darling, I couldn't make it down the stairs, let alone up the street."

"You've been hitting that bottle pretty hard, haven't you?"

"I'm going to get plastered. I'm going to sleep for two whole days and forget about everything."

"You're plastered already."

She threw out her hand and smiled foolishly. "I am not. There's a whole half bottle left. And if you're a good boy," she added, "I might let you have one teeny little drink out of it."

After ten cans of beer Rocky's appetite for drink was sharpened rather than dulled and, since he couldn't go out himself and Jenny was in no condition to, he had no choice. He would have one drink, he decided. Two at the most.

It was dark when he finished. The bottle was empty, and he lay cold on the divan. Jenny went over and shook him hard. His face twitched and he grunted, but he didn't open his eyes.

She went to the dresser, creamed her face, put on makeup and combed her hair, then slipped into a fresh summer dress and stood there briefly, admiring her reflection in the mirror. With twelve thousand dollars she could put on a front and, given a little luck, perhaps snare the right man. Someday her picture might even appear on the society page too. A whole new life lay ahead of her and she intended to make it a good one.

She emptied the dresser drawers and placed most of the contents in a small weekend bag along with her cosmetics. Then, after she had packed the rest of her clothes in a much larger suitcase, she hurried to the closet, took down the briefcase containing the money and the silencer-equipped gun and emptied it on the bed. Working quickly, she put four hundred dollars into her wallet and the rest of the money into the weekend bag. She left the empty briefcase and the gun lying on top of the bed, took her keys from her purse and locked both suitcases.

She had just put the keys back into her purse and snapped it shut when she heard a sound and looked up. Rocky was raising himself on his elbow. His eyes were bloodshot and dangerous, his face contorting with rage.

"You lousy little tramp!" he said.

She stood paralyzed as he got to his feet and took an unsteady step forward.

"You stinking little bum!" he snarled, closing his fists. "Gonna walk out with everything, were you, and leave me stranded?"

Breaking the spell, she sprang forward and picked up the gun, raised it and pulled the trigger. The bullet caught Rocky in the chest. A dark red splotch appeared on his shirt as if by magic. But he still came forward, staggering, lurching, his arms extended. She fired again. He sagged backwards. In a few seconds he was dead.

Even the two dull pings had seemed to fill the room and overflow outside. She hurried to the window and peered down as if expecting to find a throng of people looking up. The alley was empty. A piano thumped in a nearby barroom and on the floor below a television blared.

With a breath of relief she picked up her suitcases and purse, turned out the light and left the apartment.

Locking the door behind her, she hurried down two flights of stairs and stepped out into the street.

It was four blocks to Bourbon Street and the milling crowds of tourists that filled it, like an endless, undulating serpent, always active, always moving. Picking her way through this mass of humanity, she continued for another two blocks to the nearest drugstore. She went to the phone booth and called the airport, requesting a reservation on the first flight to Los Angeles, any airline, any class.

She was told that everything was booked up until next day. "I can get you a seat on the 9:10 flight tomorrow morning," the clerk said and, since she had no choice in the matter, she accepted.

When he asked for her name she blurted out the first one that came to her. It seemed she must use any name but her own, and once it was spoken it could not be retracted.

She spent the night at a hotel on St. Charles Avenue and the next morning she took a cab to the airport, arriving there almost an hour early. She wore a smart, tailored suit and white high-heeled shoes and, with the little pillbox straw pushed back on her head, she looked very chic.

She paid for her ticket and checked in the large suitcase, explaining to the clerk that she intended to carry the small one. "May I leave it here until departure time?"

"Certainly."

He took the bag and handed her a baggage check. She dropped the plane ticket into her purse and put the baggage check in her wallet, wondering what the clerk would think if he knew the value of the suitcase he had just stored under the counter.

As she walked away she noticed two men who seemed to be observing her with interest. She continued past them, her high-heeled shoes tap-tapping on the terazzo floor, toward the main entrance. Suddenly she had the feeling they were following her.

She paused on the concrete walk outside the door, looking all around, with the bored indifference of the seasoned traveler about to embark upon another routine trip, but a slight paleness and a certain tenseness in her face disputed her otherwise casual appearance.

Then it happened. The two men moved up to her and the stout one said, "Police officers," and pulled out his wallet. He flipped it open to expose something that she could not quite see, then closed it and put it back in his pocket. "You'll have to come with us."

She looked into his plump red face incredulously, her mind in turmoil. How? How could they possibly have discovered Rocky's body so soon? And how could they have traced her with such apparent ease?

"But why?" she stammered.

"You'll find that out later," he said in a grave tone. "Please come along."

"But my plane—" she protested.

"You needn't worry about that. We'll take care of everything."

They got into a car. Jenny sat in back with the stout, red-faced man, while the other one drove. They turned right on the Airline Highway, heading away from the city instead of toward it.

Jenny looked at him in alarm. "Where are we going?"

The man didn't answer. He had lighted a cigarette and now he sat back, studiously puffing on it, holding it in a peculiar way between his thumb and forefinger as if it were a dangerous thing.

"This isn't the way to New Orleans," Jenny exclaimed.

"Calm yourself. Easy does it."

The driver turned and gave her a quick look but he said nothing.

Then it suddenly dawned on her that these men were not what they claimed to be. "Who are you?" she demanded. "What do you want?"

"Mrs. Devereux," the stout man said in a patient

voice, "you're a nice girl and a pretty girl. But you talk too much. Why don't you just sit back and enjoy the scenery. We know what we're doing."

Then she understood. These two strange men, whoever they were, had mistaken her for the real Mrs. Devereux. It all came back to her, Rocky's voice reading out loud, *It goes on to say she's taking a trip to the Coast to visit her old man who's a stockbroker out there.*

She almost laughed. The whole thing was unbelievable, fantastic, an outlandish coincidence. The real Mrs. Devereux was leaving too, that same morning, perhaps on another plane. In some way the men had known about it and they had been there waiting.

The same two questions echoed in her brain again. Why? Who were they? There was something sinister about them; she knew it now. The answers came to her like a shock. They were kidnapers. They were going to hold her for ransom.

In a way it was hilarious; in another way terrifying.

She looked at the stout man and said, "You're making a mistake. I'm not Mrs. Devereux. My name is Jenny Wilson. I don't even know Mrs. Devereux. I saw her picture in the paper," she went on desperately, "and I'll admit that I look like her. But I'm not. Really I'm not. I'm Jenny Wilson. Don't you understand?"

The man yawned and flipped his cigarette out through the open window. He was totally unimpressed.

They had been moving at a high rate of speed. Suddenly the car slowed down and turned into a narrow road. The road crept around the border of a low marshland thick with mosquitoes. They followed it a short distance and stopped. The driver spoke for the first time.

"End of the line," he said. "Everybody out."

Jenny was still trying to reason with the man, to ex-

plain things as they really were, when he caught hold
of her arm and shoved her out. He got out, too. The
driver remained behind the wheel.

It occurred to her then that something more insidi-
ous was about to happen. She fought like a wildcat,
and the man dealt her a blow with the back of his
hand that sent her staggering backward. Through a
blur of tears she saw his hand slip under his coat and
come out with a gun.

They were professional men, thoroughly skilled in
their business. It took one bullet. She died instantly.

They dumped her body in the swamp and waited
there until the muck closed over it before they drove
away. The stout man sat beside the driver. He had
opened Jenny's purse and taken the wallet from inside. Out of the four hundred dollars there was still
almost two hundred left, along with the baggage
check.

He put the money into his pocket and said to the
driver, "She was a hellcat, wasn't she, Albert? Bit my
hand, she did."

"You wouldn't think it," Albert answered. "A rich
dame like that."

"They're all alike, rich or poor. They're all hellcats
underneath."

"Maybe that's why he wanted to get rid of her," Albert said in a thoughtful voice. "Maybe she was getting to be too much for him."

"That could be, Albert. It could very well be."

He took the baggage check out of the wallet and
tore it, slowly and methodically, into little pieces, then
held them in his fist and stuck his arm out the window. He opened his hand and the wind caught the
pieces and whipped them away, scattering them like a
trail of confetti behind the fast-moving car.

THE DOUBLE CORNER

by Philip Ketchum

Lennie Hill was a quiet and undistinguished person. He would not stand out in a crowd, not even a small crowd. He was average in size, neither tall nor short, thin nor fat. His features were quite ordinary, the eyes dark but not too dark, the nose just a nose, the mouth just a mouth, the hair mouse colored and straight. In general he seemed a little timid, one of the herd, certainly no one of importance. Actually, he was a jewel thief, and one of the best in the country.

He knew it, but no one else knew it. In his dozen years of operations, he had set no pattern which could be distinguished. There was a pattern, of course, which he followed, but it was too ordinary to be noticed, too simple to be analyzed. He always worked alone. He worked very carefully. He fit his operations into the normal background of everyday living. He never made any great, outstanding success. He never hit the top brackets, but he did very well. In the course of a normal year he might clean up fifty to sixty thousand dollars, net profit. He made no income tax returns. So far as the Bureau of Internal Revenue was concerned, Lennie Hill did not exist. There was no such person.

The range of his operations extended from Seattle to San Diego, from Miami to Boston, and a score of places in between. He kept on the move. He might stay in one town three months, handle three jobs, then move on to another town. One of his real problems was selling the jewels he picked up. He took a beating there. He realized about fifty percent of the discount value of the jewels he took, and very carefully, what he picked up in Boston, he would fence in Chicago. He was one of the most cautious in the business. He never carried a gun in his life. He was afraid of guns. Never, on the job, did he hurt anyone. Of course the people he robbed might cry to the Heavens that they had been hurt, but he would not have considered this worthy of notice. His theory was that the rich could afford to replace the jewels he took and, in a sense, his thievery was not evil—it hurt no one.

Lennie had a goal in life, a rather modest goal. He wanted to save a million dollars. With that much money he could retire and live as a gentleman for the rest of his life. He could travel, see the world. He might even get interested in some attractive girl. At the present time, he couldn't. Just as he avoided guns, he avoided women. A woman might learn too much about him, then she might talk. He had one other aversion—liquor. In his profession, clear thinking was essential. With respect to his goal he had a long distance still to go, but at least he was a quarter of the way there. In a number of savings banks he had an accumulation of better than three hundred thousand dollars. Not a bad start.

He was in a new town, and his first job, as he outlined it in his mind, was one of his old, standby routines. He used it several times a year, in different places, under different guises. This time, he decided, he would pose as a telephone repairman. A typical old uniform was not hard to find. He cleaned it himself, repaired it. He wanted to be neat, but not too neat. He would appear respectful, but he would not overdo it. He had already picked out the apartment house he would try. It was one of the new ones, exclusive enough so that only the wealthy could afford to stay here. He chose a corner apartment on one of the top floors in the back.

He selected Thursday as a good day for his venture.

Thursday, quite often, was the servants' day off. He picked eleven o'clock in the morning as the best hour. If an apartment was vacant at eleven o'clock in the morning, it would often be vacant until late in the afternoon. He needed less time but he liked to feel safe.

Lennie entered the apartment building by one of the rear doors left open for deliveries. He found the service elevator, rode it to the top floor, the seventeenth floor. There was no one in the corridor. Thus far he had met no one in the apartment building, but that was typical. In the average such place people did not throng the hallways. He walked briskly to one of the corner apartments, rang the bell, and waited.

A woman answered. She was fat, unattractive and about fifty. Lennie touched his cap, smiled, and said, "Madame, I'm from the telephone company. We are re-wiring some of the lines. I wonder if you will test your telephone and see if you can hear the dial tone."

"The—the dial tone?" the woman said.

"Yes, the buzzing sound you hear just before you dial. We have had to cut off some of the telephones. I must see if yours has been affected and is out of order."

"Oh, the buzzing sound," the woman said, and disappeared.

Lennie waited patiently in the hallway.

After a time the woman returned. "I can hear the buzzing sound. I mean, the dial tone."

"Good," Lennie said. "Then your telephone has not been cut off. I am sorry I bothered you."

"That's all right," the woman said.

Lennie walked to the other end of the corridor, tried another corner apartment. A rather young and attractive woman, dressed in a light robe, came to the door. Lennie went through the same routine about the dial tone. The woman assured him that the telephone sounded right.

Lennie walked down to the sixteenth floor, rang

the bell at one of the front corner apartments. He rang, and rang, and rang, but got no answer. Then, as quietly as he could, and as swiftly as possible, he got busy at the lock. Lennie was a wizard at locks. He knew what they were like, inside, no matter what the brand. In less than three minutes, the door was open. He stepped inside. His heart beat had picked up just a bit. This was an old game to him, but it was still exciting. It gave him a charge to do a thing like this. It was much better than a routine job, and much more profitable.

This was a nice apartment, well carpeted, well furnished, and artistically decorated; he had entered a hundred which were very much the same. They whispered to him of wealth, of affluence. Money and jewels would be around—possibly loose in a jewelcase in the bedroom—or in a wall safe not well hidden. A wall safe was always a challenge. A few had baffled him, but not many. The average wall safe might hold him up ten minutes. Most were ridiculously easy to open.

Lennie made a quick search of the apartment. No one seemed to be home. He spent a little time in the bedroom, found a jewel case in a bottom drawer, glanced through it. Most of what he found was costume jewelry, but he noticed several items which might have been of value. These pieces he dropped into his pocket. He hunted for the wall safe, found it, and laughed softly. It was a typical wall safe, beautiful to look at and safe from the prying fingers of a maid or a butler, but any man with only a fair amount of knowledge about locks could have opened it with little trouble.

He twisted the dial, listened, and suddenly he stiffened and caught his breath. A woman's voice startled him, and there was a caustic sound in what she was saying. "Try eleven, nine, one, starting to the left."

He lowered his hands, took a quick look over his shoulder. The woman stood just outside one of the clothes closets. She was young, slender, unsmiling, and she was holding a gun in her hand. The gun was pointed straight at him.

Lennie stood silent, numb. On several occasions during his nefarious career he had been nearly caught. A number of times he had been in serious danger. But never in his life had anything like this happened. Never had he been forced to look at the muzzle of a gun. The gun the woman was holding was not large, but there was death in it. He could sense it, could almost smell it.

"I am very good with a gun" she said quietly. "If I have to, I will shoot you. I am quite sure the police won't blame me."

Lennie knew that too well. He had already started to rob the apartment. In his pockets were jewels which did not belong to him. More than that, some of the tools of his profession were in his pockets. He was a trespasser, caught with his fingers dirty. He could be shot right here; the woman would never be blamed.

"Did you hear me?" the woman said.

He nodded slowly. "I—I heard you."

"Turn and face me. Very carefully, reach for your gun—toss it to the bed."

He turned toward her but shook his head. "I don't have a gun."

"You don't have a gun?"

"I never carry one."

"But you've done this before."

Lennie bit his lips. He hated to make such an admission, but he might as well. Once the police searched him they would know what his profession was.

"I said, you've done this before," the woman repeated.

"I—yes, I have."

"What's your name?" she asked.

Again he hesitated, was silent.

"You might as well tell me," the woman said. "I intend to find out."

He looked toward the door. He could dive that way, but he knew he would never make it. He could lunge at her, only he would not get that far. He could already feel the chill of a prison cell.

"What's your name?" the woman repeated.

"Lennie Hill."

Her lips twisted crookedly. "My name is Mrs. Bernice Garfield. I live here with my husband. When I heard you at the door I thought it was he. He fumbles with his key, especially after he's been drinking, which is all the time. I'm not very fond of him, but don't make any mistakes. Come any closer and I'll kill you, just like that." She snapped the fingers of her free hand.

"I won't come any closer," Lennie said.

"Good," Bernice said. She pointed with the gun. "Open the safe."

"What?"

"Open the safe. I told you the combination. Start to the left, eleven, nine, one."

"But why . . ."

"You wanted to look inside, didn't you? Go ahead."

"I don't want to look inside now. I don't think I should."

"But I want you to. Go ahead."

The cold, chilly look in her eyes made him shiver. Something about her was frightening. She was not just a woman defending her home. There was an aura of evil about her. She was small, slender, but there was strength in her too, and a sense of purpose.

Her words slapped out like blows. "Lennie, open the safe!"

He turned toward the safe, worked the combination, pulled open the door, and he thought, *I'll get it now— a bullet in the back. I'll never get away from here*. But he was wrong. There was no shooting. He looked around at Bernice.

"Notice the money," she was saying. "There's ten

thousand dollars in there. Ten thousand dollars in unmarked bills. A very nice haul, don't you think?"

"I . . . I don't know," Lennie said.

"Did you expect more?"

"I . . . Why don't you call the police?"

She shook her head. "I don't want the police. Of course, if I have to I will call the police, but if I do that, you will be on the floor—very dead. I don't want to shoot you if I don't have to."

"You mean you're going to let me go?" Lennie gasped.

"Ummmm, not exactly. Don't you want the money in the safe? It's yours, if you'll do something for me."

There was the hook, and honestly, he was not surprised at the way things were developing. He mumbled his answer. "What do you want me to do?"

"Steal something."

She smiled as she said that, but it was a hard smile, thin, tight, sardonic. There was a warning in it. His skin got clammy. He said, "Steal something?"

"That's your business, isn't it? I'm not asking you to do anything unusual."

He frowned at her. "What do you want me to steal?"

"Some papers. That's all. They are in a wall safe which is much like this one. Do you think you could open it?"

"I might be able to." He was thinking quickly. What she was asking looked very easy. Too easy. There would be a complication somewhere along the line. He could see it ahead, vague and undefined, but definitely a problem. He had the intuitive feeling that nothing she told him would be true.

"Where are the papers?" he asked slowly.

"Halfway across town, in an apartment house like this."

"How will I get in?"

"You got in here."

He was still frowning. "Whose apartment is it?"

"My mother-in-law's."

"Your mother-in-law's? I don't think I understand."

She laughed briefly. "You don't have to understand. All you have to do is gain entrance to the apartment, open a wall safe, and take out some papers you'll find there, give them to me. It's as simple as that."

"Nothing in this business is simple," Lennie said, and he definitely meant it.

"I doubt if we'll have any trouble," Bernice said. "Shall we go?"

"You mean now?"

"Why not?"

"And you are going with me?"

"Of course I am, but before we go, empty your pockets. You took some jewelry. I don't think that was nice."

Lennie moved to the side of the bed. He emptied his pockets, then leaving the jewelry on the bed, he put the other things back into his pocket. From the other side of the bed, Bernice watched him narrowly.

"All right," she said, nodding. "Now, pick up the jewelry and put it in the safe, then close and lock the safe."

Lennie reached for the jewelry. "You said I could have the money in the safe."

"That comes later—after we finish at my mother-in-law's," Bernice said, and her eyes were mocking him.

He put the jewelry in the safe, closed it and locked it, and he knew he would never get his hands on this safe again. This woman was not the kind to give up even a half dollar. If there were ten thousand dollars in the safe, she would keep it there. She had shown it only as bait.

"I'll slip on a coat, then we'll go," Bernice said.

"That gun . . ." Lennie started.

"It will be in my pocket."

"If I promise. . . ."

She shook her head and laughed. "I don't want any promises. I want performance, and I'll get it. You see,

I'm not afraid of guns. If you try anything . . . but you won't, will you Lennie?"

"Put the gun in your pocket and leave it there," he muttered. "I'll do the job you want."

They left her apartment, and this time he wished someone had seen them together. They took the service elevator to the basement garage, walked to her car. An attendant noticed her from a distance. He came no closer after she called to him and said they were taking the car. She ordered Lennie to drive.

He drove the car in the direction she suggested, stopped and parked it when she told him to. They got out and walked about two blocks. He was not surprised when Bernice said, "We'll take the servants' entrance and the service elevator. There's no point in being noticed."

"You learn too quickly," he answered gruffly.

She shrugged. "I'm not a nice person—or maybe you've guessed."

They took the elevator to the ninth floor and stopped at a door marked 9-C. Lennie pressed the buzzer. There was no answer. He tried it again, then again.

"She's not home," Bernice said. "I told you on the way here that she was away."

"A man's got to be sure," he muttered, and then he got busy on the lock. It took him less than two minutes.

"Wonderful," Bernice said, as they stepped into the apartment. "Maybe I'll keep you around. This is fun." Her eyes were bright, excited.

He could sense the tension that gripped her. "Where's the safe?" he asked bluntly.

"In the bedroom. I'll show you."

He closed and locked the door to the corridor, then followed her to the bedroom. She moved the picture which hid the wall safe. She was breathing fast. She was even perspiring.

Lennie walked toward the wall safe, looked at it,

recognized the type and make. It was one that he could open very easily. He wondered what was going to happen after he opened the safe. That was a rough question. If Bernice wanted to, she could shoot him the moment he opened the safe, then she could take the papers she wanted and disappear. His death might be a mystery to the police, but that offered him little comfort.

"Hurry up, Lennie," Bernice ordered. "Hurry up. Open the safe."

He nodded, started working on it, and in less than two minutes he had solved it. But he did not try the door. He was not yet ready.

"Hurry up, Lennie," Bernice whispered.

"I'm trying," he growled. "Give me more time."

"Hurry up."

He looked around at her. "What happens . . . after I open the safe?"

"Nothing. You can go."

"Just like that?"

"Just like that, unless you want to go home with me and collect your ten thousand. I'm playing square with you, Lennie."

He was silent for a moment. Maybe she meant it. He hesitated for a moment, then twisted the dial, pulled the door open.

"You've done it, Lennie. You've done it." She was unquestionably excited. "Reach inside. See if you can find a Manila envelope with my name on it."

He reached into the safe, found the Manila envelope. He held it out toward her.

Her face was glowing. "This is it, Lennie. It's worth everything to me. I'm awfully glad you showed up this morning. I was feeling desperate. Now, if you could do one more thing for me."

Lennie shook his head instantly. "Never. I've done what you asked. Now I want to go."

Her smile was not very good. "Just one more thing for me."

"No."

She reached into her pocket, drew out her gun. Her eyes had hardened. "Just one thing, Lennie. It's a must. It can't be helped. Sit down on the edge of the bed."

He watched the gun, every muscle in his body tensed. He didn't want to sit down on the edge of the bed. He was thinking again—*Here it comes! I'll never get away from here. I'm a dead man—as dead as they come.*

Bernice pointed once more to the bed. "Sit down, Lennie. We have to wait for Alice. That's my mother-in-law. She is a very unpleasant women. You won't like her any more than I do."

"I don't want to know her," Lennie said.

"Then what we have to do will be easier."

A shudder ran over his frame. "You mean—"

"Of course, Lennie." There was a harsh note in her voice. "That's been in my mind since I met you. We had to get the papers first, and now we have them. If Alice isn't around. . . ."

"I . . . I can't do it," Lennie cried.

Her smile made his skin turn clammy. "I think you can. We'll see. Isn't that a sound from the hall door?"

He waited, rigid, almost holding his breath. He watched the bedroom door, terribly afraid of what was ahead.

Footsteps brushed along the carpeted hallway. A moment later a woman stepped into the doorway. She was older than Bernice, and rather small, but she stood very straight—and she did not seem frightened at what she found in the bedroom. Her face tightened. She glared at him, then turned her attention to Bernice.

"Hello, Alice," Bernice said. "We waited for you. You told me this morning you would be home by one o'clock. It's just one o'clock."

She pointed at Lennie. "Who's he?"

"I think you might call him a safebreaker," Bernice said. "Really, he's very good." .

"Then . . . you've been in my safe?"

Bernice waved the Manila envelope. "Yes. Here are all the horrible records about me. You should have showed them to your son long ago. Now, I'm afraid it's too late."

"The records can be drawn up again."

"But not if you're not here."

Alice frowned. "You would really kill me? I knew you were bad, but not that bad."

"You forced my hand," Bernice said. "You tried to make me leave your son. Why should I do that? When he dies I will be very well situated. I am looking forward to that. You could spoil it for me."

"So you mean to kill me."

"No. Lennie will do it."

He shook his head quickly. He had gone as far as he would go. Let them call in the police if they wanted to. A prison cell would not be pleasant but it was much more preferable than a trip to the gas chamber. Murder! He had never considered such a thing, never in his life.

Bernice spoke again and her voice was high, sharp, commanding. "Go ahead, Lennie. She's not very large, not very strong. I think I would carry her to the bed, hold a pillow over her head. Are you listening, Lennie?"

"I . . . I can't do it," Lennie said.

"You've got to."

"I can't."

"Then I'll have to kill you both—make it look as though you were robbing the apartment. Too bad, Lennie. Is that the way you want it?"

He shuddered, tried to swallow the lump in his throat. He took a quick look at Bernice. She was as hard as she sounded. If she had to, she would do just what she had said, shoot them both. He took a glance at the other woman, Alice. There was nothing soft about her. Her face had hard angles, deep buried eyes. She probably was not much nicer than Bernice, but if he had to make a choice, he would turn to her.

"Lennie, I'm waiting." Bernice snapped the words at him.

He gulped, moistened his lips. "Do I have to?"

"Yes, Lennie."

He had to circle the foot of the bed where Bernice was standing, and he circled behind her, toward Alice. But he did not go that far. He stopped as he was passing Bernice. He reached up and closed both hands around her throat. She uttered a gasping cry, then she started struggling, and it was not easy to hold her. She was wiry, strong, and she almost got away. But she didn't. Eventually she grew silent.

They were on the floor by this time and, when Lennie let her go, she did not move. Her face was blotched, ugly to look at.

"I am afraid she is dead," Alice said, "And I can't say that I'm sorry. She has just been waiting for my son to die."

Lennie sat up. He was glad of the choice he had made—Bernice instead of Alice, but this was a horrible experience. It would take him a long time to get over it.

Alice picked up the gun Bernice had dropped. She was examining it curiously. "I couldn't get away from her," Lennie said. "She made me come here. She threatened to call the police. I had to do what she told me to."

"Yes. I know." Alice said. "You didn't have a chance. You still don't."

Lennie's eyes widened. "I . . . I don't know what you mean?"

"This has to be explained to the police," Alice said. "In some way or other I have to account for a dead body—Bernice. The easiest way is like this." She was pointing the gun at him, straight at him, and she was not smiling. She looked quite serious.

"Wait!" Lennie cried. "Wait. I didn't. . . ."

"I'm sorry, but it has to be this way," Alice said. She pulled the trigger.

It was rather strange but, as she was firing the gun, she looked very much like Bernice.

THE SCIENTIST AND THE EXTERMINATOR

by Arthur Porges

El Supremo, Luis Alvarez Ybarra, was dead, and Lieutenant Trask, who bore little of the onus for the general's sudden demise, mourned him not as a fellow human—few would be that compassionate—but purely as symbolic of an embarrassing blunder. The deceased was also known as "The Butcher of Corona Del Norte," which accounts for many dry eyes in his native land.

Most of the black marks in the unfortunate matter went to the FBI, with a few demerits left for the State Department, since it was mainly the business of these two well-funded organizations to protect foreign dignitaries.

"Don't quote me," the detective said blandly. "A good cop isn't supposed to condone homicide, and I've never done it before. Or hardly ever," he added, being an honest man. "But the extermination of Ybarra hardly strikes me as a terrible crime. He was a mass-murderer himself, and worse, a torturer who loved his work. But I do hate not knowing just how it was done, which is why I'm here bothering you again."

Cyriack Skinner Grey, settling deeper into his wheelchair, smiled. "I can understand your feelings," he said, cocking his massive head in a typically quizzical way. "An exceptionally intriguing case, judging from the newspaper accounts."

Trask hesitated, then said rather diffidently, "What picture did you get from their stories over the last few days? Mind telling me?"

"Not at all—why should I? It'll save you from re-hashing the whole thing." He pressed a button on the arm of the chair, obtained a small mug of coffee, and handed it to his guest. It was a special blend of Kona, dark and heavy. For himself, he pushed something the detective couldn't see, and came up with a small, greenish apple. "Like 'em tart," he said, taking a bite. "I'd better do it chronologically, so I can organize my thoughts and remember all the significant points. To begin with, Ybarra was supposed to stay for a week, and came for an operation, not at all dangerous, but very tricky. His hearing was failing, and we have a sur-geon who specializes in correcting the calcification of the tiny bones involved. It's such delicate work he uses a microscope and minuscule implements.

"He was given a room in the Grant Hotel with top security. That meant the rooms above, below, and on all sides were kept vacant. There were guards in the corridors watching his door and the others, too—the ones for empty rooms.

"Outside, the hotel was also closely guarded on four sides, day and night. Finally, there was a man on the roof at all times.

"Nevertheless, on the night before his move to the hospital, somebody managed to introduce a large amount of cyanide gas into the room. Ybarra was in bed, asleep apparently, and didn't know what killed him. Some would say," Grey added in a hard voice, "he got off too easy. But there it is: a room nine floors up, with six more over it, maximum security in every conceivable way, yet he was killed."

"You have the facts right," Trask said. "But there's just a bit more. We even have the empty gas cylinder; it was found in a trash can two blocks from the hotel. And to top that, we know where the killer operated from—a room in another hotel across the street—but it's almost fifty feet away, although at about the same height as Ybarra's. But how he got a cylinder weighing ten pounds across from his window to the Hotel Grant one . . ." Here the lieutenant shook his head in wonder.

"Did you also find out where he got the gas?"

"That was easy. A pest-control outfit was burglarized some days ago. Good choice; maybe the only one. Not many places keep cyanide around. 'Bug-Out Exterminators'—there's a name for you!"

"How did you identify the killer's room?" Grey asked, dropping his apple core into a slot.

"Routine matter. We checked everybody who rented a room there since Ybarra came. Of several possibles, only one looked like a Latin American, and in his room, which he took by the way, as 'James Carillo'— not his real name, of course—we found clippings about Ybarra, left there, I think, just to taunt us. Why he didn't leave the gas container, too, I don't know; but neither did he try very hard to dispose of it effectively; wanted us to find that as well. One of your political, radical-idealist types, no doubt; proud of the murder."

"How was the gas introduced?"

"Nobody knows," Trask admitted. "I didn't get to see the room right away. You know the FBI; they look down on cops. Well, they think it was either the ventilator or the air-conditioner—what the hell else could it be, with a guard at the door?—but don't really know which, if either. I forgot to mention that to prevent a sniper from the hotel across the street, there were not only heavy draperies inside Ybarra's window, but a chicken-wire cover outside, just in case somebody tried to toss a grenade or bomb in—on the ninth floor, mind you! What from, a helicopter? To install it they had to use a sort of window-cleaner's scaffold setup."

"Did it also cover the air-conditioner you mentioned? It was a window type, wasn't it?"

"Yes. Tricky business. Had to have a bulge to go over the intake part, which sticks out about eight inches."

"In a way," the scientist said, "security helped do Ybarra in. I understand that the guard at his door smelled bitter almonds and knocked, but naturally the locks were all set and he couldn't get in until much too late."

"That's true, but if he had got in we might have two bodies; the room was loaded, we're told. The FBI people backed well off to let the air clear. Bad stuff, cyanide gas."

"Well," Grey said, "the facts so far are simply not adequate for a highly probable inference. I need more data."

"Like what?" Trask asked eagerly.

"Did you check the air-conditioner thoroughly?"

"The FBI did, and found nothing of interest. They had hoped to find some kind of time-delay canister inside, I suspect; that would have cleared up the matter—to a point. Anyhow, I looked it over when they finally condescended to permit it. Didn't find anything."

"It doesn't take much," the scientist said. "Suppose you could bring me the filter?"

"Probably. Although it was pretty dirty; should have been changed long ago. But the Grant Hotel is starting to cut corners; maybe too much modern competition. Newer places, for example, have central air-conditioning. Do you have an idea?" he added wistfully.

"Not really, but something in the filter might suggest one."

"Then I'll bring it, even if the room's rented now. As I said, a change is in order, anyhow."

"While you're at it," Grey said, "take a good look at the outside screen."

Trask blinked. "What for?"

"I'm not sure. Maybe a dent; but it could be just a spot where the paint, if any, is chipped." He raised an admonitory hand, smiling. "No use asking questions; I'm just 'hunting,' as they say, about a feedback setup trying to stabilize. I'll say this much: I suspect the gas came in by the air-conditioner, but it's only a hunch or quasi-reasonable guess based on the Holmes axiom—you know the one—other possibilities too impossible, so the highly-improbable is favored!"

The detective looked at him wordlessly. "I can't even comment sensibly on that," he said in a plaintive voice. "I'll be back with the filter and a reconditioned brain, obviously needed around here!" and he stalked out.

Moments later, rather sheepishly, he returned. "Forgot to give you the file—what there is. Not very much, and little you don't already know; but the photos may help."

"Good," Grey said. "I'll go through it."

The scientist studied the material in a way oddly desultory for him; his mind seemed to be elsewhere. Actually, he was convinced circumstances were so limiting that a solution ought to suggest itself even at this point, assuming one had enough imagination. From one room to another, fifty feet away, both about ninety feet high—that was the crux of the puzzle, even with no additional data. But a heavy cylinder—ten pounds Trask had said—across such a gap and without elaborate or massive equipment, no way . . .

He examined the photos. Only one seemed to interest him; it showed that the area between the two hotels was actually a small park; that could be significant. Late at night, when the murder was accomplished, few, if any, people would be around. It also implied a degree of darkness; the killer could do—well, whatever he did—those nine stories up with little chance of being observed; in fact, his entire operation might be totally invisible from so far below in such circumstances. Noise, of course, was another matter. How could he get the gas cylinder across in relative silence?

Dead stop. He pressed a button in the arm of his chair, and when the little crystal goblet of old brandy proffered itself, raised it to his lips even as they twitched briefly. Cure your delusions of infallibility!

he admonished himself. James Carillo is too clever for
yours truly. Smiling, he sipped, savoring the excellent
liquor. Then it was back to the dossier, and the baf-
fling puzzle that had produced it . . . But after two
more hours he was still without answers. Sighing, he
gave up the riddle for that day.

The filter, once Grey had a chance to examine it,
proved a familiar type, consisting of glass wool supported by a rectangular frame. It was quite dirty, but
not clogged, so on that warm night—Ybarra's last—the
general would have had no reason to fiddle with the
cooler.

The wool was mostly dark gray, but city air can do
that in hours. There were, however, scattered patches
of black. It was in one of these that Grey found something of interest. He picked at it with tweezers; a shred
of black, shiny stuff, nearly invisible in the soiled fi-
bers of the filter. The scientist studied it with growing
excitement. The theater of his mind, with imagination
as the seasoned producer, came to life. Damn the gas
tank; its weight was no longer an obstacle to a convincing theory; now it was only a matter of journey-
man work, mere implementation of the basic concept,
a brilliant one, Grey thought, with admiration.

When Trask came back for a briefing, the scientist
made no attempt to conceal his elation. He held up
the scrap of material, and said, "Here's what fooled us.
It's polyethylene, the stuff they make weather balloons
from. Carillo didn't need to transport a heavy cylinder
across to Ybarra's room—just a balloon full of gas!"

The lieutenant blinked, then smiled approval, but
his reaction seemed subdued.

"That makes a difference," he admitted, "but still,
getting anything across there is more than I can figure
out."

"I won't say it was done this way," Grey said, "but
here's how it could be accomplished—how I'd do it.

"Start with a small, powerful magnet, alnico type; weight about an ounce. Fasten a short wire around it with the free end having a loop, to serve as a pulley. Now take a hundred feet of fishing line, monofilament, light and strong, say two-pound test weight, and pass one end through the wire loop. With the two free ends at his window, Carillo projects the magnet against the wire mesh near—just above, he'd hope—the air-conditioner."

"Wait a minute," Trask interrupted. "What do you mean 'project'? How?"

"Can't say for sure. One way would be a good modern slingshot. Or with a dowel fastened to the magnet, you could use an air rifle. There are many ways. Probably we'll never know which was used. But, to go on, Carillo now has a sort of endless clothesline running to Ybarra's window, once he ties his two ends together. All right; he fills the balloon with cyanide gas from the cylinder—very carefully, I'd assume!—ties it to the filament, and by pulling on the line moves the balloon over to the general's window. There he pops it; the released gas is sucked into the cooler's grille, and that's the end of Ybarra."

"Slow down," the lieutenant pleaded. "How does he pop the balloon?"

"Same answer," was the airy reply. "He could have used the slingshot, firing a ball bearing. Or the air gun with a BB or .22 pellet. Easy, compared to sending the magnet and line across. I suggest," he added, "a search, probably futile, for the evidence."

"Which will be?" Trask asked in a dry voice.

"After the balloon collapses, Carillo would naturally pull on the fishing line. But the chunk of polyethylene, minus the fragment I found in the filter, was bound to jam at the magnet; too bulky for any loop. So that end would fall down to the park. He could easily reel the magnet and empty balloon up to his window, but that might attract somebody's notice, and why should he bother? If he didn't, they should be still somewhere in the brush. By the way, did you check the wire mesh?"

"Yes," the detective said, eyes twinkling. "There was a mark or slight dent, all right. Made by the magnet, I suppose."

"I'd say so. Must have made quite a thump to go all that way carrying a double line; but with Ybarra asleep and not hearing well to begin with . . . Otherwise, he might have investigated and still be alive."

"It's a wonder nobody saw anything, what with a big balloon moving across from one window to another."

"Little chance of that. It was the middle of the night, dark, an empty park, other guests probably sleeping; and ninety feet up, remember. Besides, the balloon was black; he used some kind of paint or dye; didn't miss a trick, Mr. Carillo!"

"I'll have the park area searched," Trask said.

So it was that some hours later he returned with a crumpled mass of polyethylene to which was still attached a magnet and six inches of monofilament line.

"Evidently got snagged in the shrubbery," the detective said. "Carillo either couldn't find it in the dark or didn't bother, as you suggested. Hauled in what broke loose, I suppose, and took off like a big-bottomed bird. Our hope of identifying him, much less finding him, is nil."

"I'm not too sad about that, are you?" Grey asked, smiling. "Considering his means—cyanide gas—and the character of Ybarra, you might think of it as a kind of amateur, free-lance job of pest extermination."

"Unofficially," Trask said, "I agree. Officially, no comment."

BORDER CROSSING

by James Holding

Soon Fat was the proprietor of the best Chinese restaurant in Montreal.

His name, promising as it did the early correction of his own natural emaciation, gave rise, of course, to a certain amount of hilarity among his English-speaking patrons. Furthermore, the name (which is no more hilarious to a Chinese than the name Smith is to an American) was a definite business asset, an advertising come-on. What diner, with a sense of humor and a weight problem, could resist coming to Soon Fat's restaurant to feast on delicious Chinese food that was actually more likely to make him soon thin than soon fat?

Soon Fat was Canadian-born, fluent in both English and French, the shrewd son of immigrant parents, now dead, and a leader in Montreal's Chinese community. All this was generally known. What was not generally known, however, was Soon Fat's deep personal interest in improving the unhappy lot of certain of his fellow Orientals.

Ah Lee was one such case.

At 10:15 on a Thursday evening in January—a blustery, overcast night of penetrating cold outdoors—Ah Lee sat alone over a pot of tea at an inconspicuous table at the rear of Soon Fat's restaurant. He watched with anxious eyes the comings and goings of Soon Fat about his host's duties: welcoming customers, chatting with habitués, urging waitresses to faster service, taking drink orders, popping in and out of the swinging kitchen doors on mysterious errands.

At length, when one of Soon Fat's passages across his dining room brought him close to his table, Ah Lee seized the opportunity to address him shyly. "The wind from the east veers into the south," he said in an uncertain voice, speaking in the Cantonese dialect.

Soon Fat raised his eyebrows in surprise and stopped beside Ah Lee. "Did you say something to me, young man?" he asked in English. "Something about the east wind?"

Ah Lee regarded Soon Fat in bewilderment and said nothing. His mouth hung open.

Soon Fat sat down in the other chair at Ah Lee's table and smiled affably at him as though he had known him all his life. He repeated his question, this time in French. "Did you say something to me, young man? Something about the east wind?"

Again he got the blank look, slowly changing to one of acute anxiety. Ah Lee then revealed in Cantonese the reason for his bewilderment. "Do you not understand our mother tongue?" he asked.

Soon Fat smiled with his lips held tightly together. "Of course," he said easily, in Cantonese. "But it is evident that you do not understand English or French."

"Oh!" Ah Lee's features rearranged themselves into an expression of relief. "That is true, sir."

"OK. Now that we have that settled, what's all this business about the east wind veering into the south?" Soon Fat asked him.

"Kai San in Hong Kong—" Ah Lee began.

Soon Fat held up a slender hand. "No names, please," he said, smiling as though cracking a joke with Ah Lee. He was a very careful man. Who knew when one of his late customers might grow curious about a serious conversation between Soon Fat and a strange Chinese?

"Very well, sir. I was told to introduce myself to you by using that phrase."

"You want my help, eh?"

Ah Lee looked at his hands and saw they were trembling. He clasped them together on the tablecloth to stop their quivering. "Yes," he said in a low voice. "Yes, sir. I need your help. Please."

Speaking rapidly in a voice inaudible ten feet away, Soon Fat said, "All right. Finish your tea, pay your check, and go outside like a regular customer leaving. Understood? Then walk left around the nearest corner to the mouth of an alley that runs behind this building. Go up the alley till you come to the back of this restaurant. You'll know it by a fan in the back wall of my kitchen. Come into the kitchen through the rear door, mount the staircase to your right, go into the room at the top of the staircase to your left. It is my office. Wait there in the dark for me. I will not be long."

Ah Lee said, "What of your chefs?"

"They're my nephews. They see nothing. Take care, however, that no one else sees where you go." Soon Fat stood up and hurried to the front of the restaurant to say good night to a group of departing diners.

Ah Lee finished his pot of tea, feeling relief and, at last, genuine hope. When he rose from his table, he left no tip for his waitress. Walking to the cashier's desk to pay his check, his worn sandals, with one thong broken, scuffed along the tile floor. He wore faded jeans with ragged bottoms, and under his open black Windbreaker, a soiled white T-shirt obviously turned inside out to present its cleaner side.

He paid for his tea and left the restaurant, following Soon Fat's instructions exactly. He negotiated the corner, found the alley mouth, slipped into it as quietly as possible. When he located the rear of Soon Fat's restaurant by the whirring of the large fan set into the back wall of the kitchen, he crouched in the shadow of stacked garbage cans for a time, listening and watching intently for signs that he was observed. After five minutes, he decided he was not.

The restaurant's rear door was unlocked. He opened it quietly, stepped inside, and looked somewhat fearfully about him at the spotless stainless-steel kitchen where Soon Fat's excellent cuisine was born. Two young Chinese in high white hats were chatting by the huge electric range. They raised their eyes and looked at him without interest, then went back to their animated conversation. Ah Lee thought he heard several girls' names mentioned amid laughter.

He looked to his right. A closed door was there. Ah Lee took two rapid steps, twisted the doorknob, pulled the door open and eeled through it. When he closed it behind him he found himself in impenetrable darkness.

He stretched out his hands before him, stooping, and felt the risers of a flight of stairs. Straightening, he found a stair rail and mounted the steps, guiding himself by the banister under his hand. The stairs were steep. When the banister ended, he knew he had reached the top. He felt left and discovered door panels. He opened the door and inched through it. He never remembered such darkness. It was like being blind.

He closed the door silently behind him. Three steps into the gloom and his shinbone came in painful contact with what his seeking hands told him was the edge of a straight wooden chair. He sighed gratefully, sank into the chair, put his feet together, and waited patiently for Soon Fat.

Soon Fat must be able to see in the dark like a cat and move as quietly, Ah Lee thought, for although he heard no footsteps on the staircase, heard no door open, felt no movement of air, he suddenly felt Soon Fat's hand on his shoulder. Ah Lee started violently, sucking in his breath.

A chuckle and the hand was withdrawn from his shoulder. Immediately, a rose-colored lamp flashed on behind Ah Lee's back. After the total darkness, the light made him blink, and when his vision cleared, he saw Soon Fat smiling his tight-lipped smile at him from behind a dainty teakwood desk. The smile, Ah Lee was sure, held a hint of malicious pleasure at having startled his guest with that shoulder touch in the dark.

The room was sparsely furnished. Two other straight chairs, like the one on which Ah Lee sat, flanked a crimson sofa on the wall opposite the doorway. These, with the desk, desk chair, three lamps, were the only furniture in the room. Now, however, the shaded lamps showed Ah Lee that the chairs and desk were beautifully embellished by hand-carved bas-reliefs of horsemen, dragons and demons; that the bases of the lamps looked very much like twelve-hundred-year-old Tang pottery. An oval Chinese rug covered the floor and pleated black draperies masked the walls solidly save for the doorway at the top of the staircase. There wasn't a sign of a window anywhere. The room was comfortably warm, but Ah Lee saw no heating source. A telephone occupied the exact center of Soon Fat's desk top, flanked on one side by an appointment pad, on the other by a ball-point pen in an exquisite white onyx holder.

It was a simple room but rich and dramatic enough to remind Ah Lee forcibly, by contrast, of his own poverty and desperation.

Soon Fat said, "You like it? My office?"

"It is beautiful," said Ah Lee sincerely.

Soon Fat dismissed it with a wave of his hand. "It is private, at least. And I take it you are interested in privacy now?" He giggled.

Ah Lee nodded. "Kai San said you would help me."

Soon Fat bowed deeply, not an easy thing to do when seated behind a desk. "I am at your service. May I know your name?"

"Ah Lee."

"And you want me to help you do what?"

"To get into the United States," Ah Lee said.

"So. Where do you come from?"

"Hong Kong."

"How did you come here?"

"On the *Kowloon Star*. As a deckhand." Ah Lee remembered the long weeks of brutal labor he had put in aboard the *Kowloon Star* before that rusty freighter had finally wallowed its way across the Gulf of St. Lawrence and nosed into the St. Lawrence River.

"You jumped ship?" Soon Fat asked.

"Yes, sir. Four days ago."

Soon Fat opened a drawer of his desk and withdrew a thin sheaf of newspaper clippings, held together by a paper clip. He leafed through them rapidly. Then, "Here we are," he said. "The *Kowloon Star*. Yes, it docked here Monday." He gave Ah Lee an apologetic look. "I keep these shipping news items purely as a measure of security, you understand."

Ah Lee said with dignity, "I do not lie, sir."

"Perhaps not. But some of my charges do. And I must be very careful." Soon Fat put away his clippings, watching Ah Lee all the while with an expression of reprimand on his narrow face. "So for my own protection, Ah Lee, I shall check to see if a Chinese deckhand named Ah Lee was a member of the crew of the *Kowloon Star* . . . and jumped ship here in Montreal last Monday."

Ah Lee was penitent. "I am sorry, sir. I understand you must take precautions."

Soon Fat's good humor was restored at once. "Actually," he said lightly, "my 'help' as you call it, is officially frowned upon. The authorities insist on regarding it as the illegal smuggling of aliens into our great sister country across the border." Soon Fat drew back his lips in a sour grin that gave Ah Lee a glimpse of elegant bonewhite false teeth. "Where do you wish to go in the United States?"

"I have two cousins in New York," Ah Lee answered, excitement flushing his cheeks. "They wrote my father asking if I could come to America and live with them. They promise to teach me the American language very quickly . . . so that I can work in their tailor shop. I do not wish to sound conceited, sir, but I am a very good tailor. I worked for eight years at Hallmark Tailors in Kowloon . . ."

"No doubt," Soon Fat said dryly. "Do you mean New York City?"

"Yes, sir."

Soon Fat nodded and made a note on his appointment pad with the ball-point pen. Then he looked up and said suddenly, "How did you learn of Kai San?"

"He is my father's friend," Ah Lee returned simply. "He told my father that you have generously helped many of our countrymen into the United States. And he gave me the phrase about the east wind as a . . . a . . . password to you." Ah Lee sighed passively.

"I see." Soon Fat chuckled. "I am famous in Hong Kong, eh?" He tapped his fingernails on the top of his desk. "Well, these smuggling tricks, alas, cost money, Ah Lee. Much money."

"I have money," Ah Lee volunteered eagerly, sensing that Soon Fat had now decided to help him. "My life savings, sir. And a little money besides, that my father could spare, now that he is very old."

"How much?" asked Soon Fat bluntly.

Ah Lee opened his mouth to answer, then shut it again out of native caution. "How much is your price?" he countered cautiously.

To his surprise, Soon Fat laughed aloud. "I see you are not the young fool I took you for, Ah Lee."

Ah Lee couldn't help smiling, too. "I meant no offense, sir."

"Do you have twelve hundred dollars?"

Ah Lee gasped at the amount. So much! He temporized. "Hong Kong dollars?"

"Canadian," Soon Fat said evenly.

"It is a fortune!" Ah Lee moaned. "A fortune!"

"Half of it goes to my American colleague in our enterprise," Soon Fat explained peremptorily.

"It is still a great fortune!" Ah Lee mourned, but he began the traditional bargaining eagerly. In the end, they settled on a thousand dollars, the thousand to include the price of Ah Lee's bus ticket to New York City.

Soon Fat watched politely as Ah Lee counted out the Canadian dollars for which he had exchanged his entire store of yen before leaving Hong Kong. Then Soon Fat gathered up the bills, tapped them against the desk top to even their edges. "Return here at midnight tomorrow night," he instructed Ah Lee. "Come in the rear entrance as you did tonight. Make sure you are not observed. And bring your luggage with you. My American colleague will pick you up here and see that you get across the border into Vermont and on your way to New York."

"I shall be here." Ah Lee breathed deeply, scarcely able to believe that his dream might actually come true. "At midnight?"

"Yes. You will be safe until then?"

Ah Lee blushed. "I think so, sir," he said. "I am staying at Madame Turot's." Madame Turot's was an obscure rooming house buried deep in the Chinese section of the city. It was also a bordello.

Soon Fat showed his false teeth again. "You young men!" he said.

Ah Lee shook his head. "Kai San also recommended Madame's to me. As a rooming house only." He gave a small grin. "I cannot afford the other services offered."

"Well," Soon Fat said, "it is a safe house, at any rate. Until tomorrow night, Ah Lee."

They bowed deeply to each other and Ah Lee took his departure. As he started to descend the staircase to Soon Fat's restaurant kitchen, he heard quite clearly through the door behind him the clicking sound of Soon Fat's telephone as he dialed a number.   —

At eleven-thirty the following night, Soon Fat was ensconced in his office over the restaurant kitchen. A pot of tea rested at his elbow on top of the teakwood desk. He drank the tea from a small porcelain cup as he talked to his visitor. "You honor me by your presence," he said formally to the man who sat in the straight chair occupied last night by Ah Lee. "I expected one of your sons."

"I might as well handle it myself this time," Roger Bailey said, nursing a shot glass full of bourbon in his rough farmer's hands. "I had to come across to see my sister in the hospital here, anyway."

"She is ill?" asked Soon Fat sympathetically. "How seriously?"

"About to die," Roger Bailey said with a bark of laughter. "The old cow."

Soon Fat did not understand Vermont humor, but he did his best to show he appreciated his guest's lack of sentiment. He put his fingers together like a tent and bowed agreeably. "We get a thousand dollars for this one," Soon Fat said.

The Vermonter wagged his head. "Not bad, Fatso, not bad. That's better than we got out of those two last Christmas, eh?"

Soon Fat assumed a lugubrious expression. "We got a very good price for them, everything considered."

Bailey grinned wolfishly. "It wasn't my fault that the Immigration boys happened to make a check of the area that night," he said, "and that I couldn't pick your two Chinks up as promised after they walked across the border. When I got the tip-off about the border check, it was too late to do anything. No sense risking our operation for a couple of dumb Chinamen."

Soon Fat said softly, "I am sorry what happened to them. They were nice boys."

"So they froze to death waiting for me," Bailey said indifferently. "Tough luck for them, and don't get sentimental on me!" He took a swallow of his bourbon and changed the subject. "You get cash on the barrel-head?"

Soon Fat reached across his desk, handing Bailey a number of bills. "Certainly. Five hundred dollars for Roger Bailey. Five hundred dollars for Soon Fat." He giggled.

Bailey counted the money carefully, then stuffed it into a pocket. "Easy money, Fatso." he said.

"You anticipate no difficulties this time, then?" Soon Fat's voice held a touch of asperity. He didn't like to be called Fatso.

"Not this time. The word from Immigration is that we'll be safe as houses tonight."

"Where?" asked Soon Fat.

"Derby Line. There's a lot of small, unguarded dirt roads around there. Tonight your boy can walk across the border as easy as a stroll in the park." Bailey made a quick sketch on the back of an envelope, showed it to Soon Fat. "See this? I'll put him off on this side, pick him up on the other, and get him on a bus in Burlington. No sweat. I'll see him to the bus myself if you like."

"That would be best, I think. He speaks no English."

"He won't need to. I already bought the bus ticket for him." He handed it to Soon Fat. "You tell him to keep his lip buttoned till he gets to New York and nobody'll bother him."

"I'll tell him."

"You better explain to him how it'll work, too. I sure can't tell him anything if he don't understand English."

"I'll explain it all to him."

"When's he due here? I want him on the seven o'clock bus tomorrow morning."

"I instructed him to come here at midnight."

"Ten more minutes," Bailey said, looking at his watch. "How about another shot while we're waiting, Fatso? That's good booze."

It was one minute to midnight when they heard Ah Lee's flapping sandals ascending the steep stairs to Soon Fat's office. There was a timid knock on the door. "Come in," Soon Fat said in Cantonese.

Ah Lee opened the door and came into the office, carrying in one hand the cheap fiberboard suitcase that held all his possessions. He looked even more bedraggled, and wearier and hungrier than the night before. There were dark circles under his eyes, staining the parchment skin.

"Good evening, Ah Lee," Soon Fat said jovially. "You rested well at Madame Turot's, I trust?"

"I could not sleep, sir. I was too happy." Ah Lee's eyes went to Roger Bailey.

"This is the American colleague I mentioned to you," Soon Fat said.

Ah Lee set down his suitcase and bowed to the American. Bailey overflowed the carved chair in which he lounged. He was massive, craggy-featured, dark-haired. His eyes were the color of dishwater and, to Ah Lee, seemed as cold as chips of ice.

Bailey said, "Hi, boy," and drained the small whiskey glass in his hand. "Go on, Fatso," he said to Soon Fat, "tell him."

Soon Fat said, "Listen carefully, Ah Lee. If you want to see New York, you must do exactly as I tell you."

Ah Lee listened attentively while Soon Fat described what was to happen to him. At the end, he smiled nervously and nodded his head. "I understand," he said. "I shall do everything you say."

"Good," said Soon Fat. Then, to Bailey, "He's ready now."

Bailey stood up, towering over Ah Lee's slight figure. He patted Ah Lee on the back with a hand like a ham. "Let's go, boy." He led the way to the door.

Ah Lee picked up his suitcase, tarried long enough to bow deeply to Soon Fat and murmur his thanks, then followed Bailey down the steep steps into the restaurant kitchen. The kitchen was dark, the restaurant closed. There were no chefs now to see Bailey lead Ah Lee through the rear door and out to the alley at the rear.

Fifty feet up the alley, a car was parked without lights. Bailey opened the trunk of this car with a key and stood back. As instructed, Ah Lee climbed into the trunk and curled up on his side, squirming about until he was as comfortable as possible. Bailey tossed his suitcase in after him and shut the trunk lid with a sharp click. Ah Lee was relieved to find that Soon Fat had told him the truth about the car trunk. The lid was sprung on one side, so that even when closed and locked, there was a half inch of space through which plenty of air could enter to prevent Ah Lee from suffocating.

For two hours, that seemed much longer, Ah Lee lay in the trunk of Bailey's car, listening to the whir and hum of the tires as they rolled over what must have been a well-paved highway, clear of snow. At first, there were half a dozen stops; Ah Lee concluded they occurred at traffic lights as Bailey made his way out of the city. After that the journey was uninterrupted until a sudden slowing, a sharp turn to the right, and a teeth-rattling jouncing over a very rough surface, indicated that the first half of his ordeal was approaching its end.

A few minutes later, the car came to a halt. Ah Lee, straining his ears, heard Bailey open his door and get out. He left the engine running. In a moment, a key rattled in the trunk lock and the lid was lifted. Bailey's massive head and shoulders loomed against a sky studded with scattered clouds and patches of stars.

"Out," Bailey said, gesturing to show Ah Lee his meaning. Ah Lee swung his legs over the edge of the trunk and stood up, stretching the cramps out of his muscles. He noticed the car was without lights. There was an inch-deep film of snow on the ground.

Ah Lee reached into the trunk and retrieved his

suitcase. Then he looked around him. They were on the edge of a wide grove of trees. Dimly in the starlight, Ah Lee could make out the single set of car tracks on the old logging road by which Bailey had reached this spot. He nodded enthusiastically at Bailey and said with a lift in his voice, "Soon Fat described this place to me," before he remembered that Bailey wouldn't understand him.

Soon Fat had described the grove of trees, the old logging track, the high hills that loomed far off to his right across the snow. Soon Fat had also explained to him very carefully that the Canadian-United States border ran right through that grove of trees and tonight it would be blessedly free of border guards. Ah Lee breathed deeply of the icy air and pulled his Windbreaker higher around his neck. He was shivering, as much from excitement as from the cold.

Bailey tapped him on the chest to get his attention, then pointed a forefinger like a dollar cigar toward the south, through the trees. "There," he said. "That way. Walk. You savvy?" He watched Ah Lee's face to make sure he understood. Ah Lee nodded again, picked up his suitcase and started to walk through the trees. They smelled deliciously fragrant, besides helping to temper the sharp wind that was trying to knife through his thin Windbreaker.

Bailey got back behind the wheel of his car and still without lights, backed, turned, and drove away up the old road to the north.

Ah Lee watched him go. He was not disturbed. Soon Fat had told him why Bailey would leave him alone for a time: Bailey would cross the border boldly and innocently, as an American citizen should, through a Customs station on a main road nearby, then double back to pick up Ah Lee at the southern edge of the grove of trees—the Vermont edge, Ah Lee thought exultantly. Soon Fat had instructed him to wait there patiently, to stay under the trees, to avoid the dirt road that bordered the grove until Bailey came to fetch him.

Ah Lee followed these instructions to the letter. He stayed inside the edge of the woods, walking up and down, flapping his arms, stamping his feet to keep his blood circulating in the piercing cold. The time passed quickly now. Ah Lee knew the worst was over.

Bailey's car appeared on the dirt road beside the woods just as the rising sun was beginning to dissipate the darkness under the trees where Ah Lee waited. Its headlights seemed pale and washed-out in the half-light of dawn. Bailey made a careful U-turn on the inch of snow, pulled to the roadside facing west, stopped, and gave a triple tap on his horn. At the signal Ah Lee picked up his suitcase and walked out from under the trees.

Less than an hour later, they came into the outskirts of an awakening Burlington. Bailey drove by back streets from the terminal, pointed to it and said, "New York. Understand? New York."

Ah Lee pulled from his pocket the bus ticket Soon Fat had given him with his instructions. "New York," he said, attempting to say the words the way Bailey said them.

Bailey grunted and motioned for him to get out of the car. When he was on the sidewalk, clutching his suitcase, Bailey pulled the car door shut and drove away without a backward glance.

Ah Lee walked into the bus terminal. He went over to the public telephone booth in the corner near the ticket office, closed himself in, and dialed a number.

A woman answered.

"Is Mr. Lehy there?" Ah Lee asked.

"I'll ring him. Hold on, Please."

In a moment, a booming bass voice came over the wire. "Yeah?" it bellowed.

"Harry?" Ah Lee asked, although he didn't need to. He recognized that stentorian shout.

"Yeah," Harry said. "Who is this?"

"Lee."

"Lee who?"

"Ah Lee Cheung."

"Oh. That Lee. Hi, Lee. You been gone so long I almost forgot about you."

"Nearly two months."

"Well, well. And how are things with you, Lee?"

"Couldn't be better. Although I'd like a hamburger and a milk shake. I'm sick and tired of fried rice and tea."

"No substance to it," Harry said, chuckling. "I know. Where are you now?"

"Bus station in Burlington. I've just been smuggled into Vermont from Canada, Harry."

"I'll be damned! Where'd you cross the border?"

"Derby Line. There wasn't a guard within a thousand miles, far as I could tell."

"That's a hell of a place there, Lee, with all those back roads and all. It's a bitch to cover."

"Maybe I can give you some information that'll make it easier," Ah Lee said, smiling to himself.

"I'd sure appreciate that."

"Start with Hong Kong. A man named Kai San Sung, a curio dealer, gave me the Canadian contact—a guy named Soon Fat in Montreal. Runs a Chinese restaurant. A smooth specimen. Charged me a thousand bucks for the trip across."

"Nice friendly feller, hey?" Harry shouted in his booming voice.

"Right. But a pussycat compared to the tiger who brought me over—a Vermonter named Roger Bailey. Owns a 1971 Skylark, Vermont license number 10-233M. Six-feet-three, heavyset, colorless eyes, dark hair, drinks bourbon straight, has a sister in a hospital in Montreal, I think, and at least two sons who help him smuggle aliens across the border after Soon Fat in Montreal sets them up." Ah Lee paused. "You getting this down?"

"I got a memory like a steel trap, Lee, you know

that. Anyway, I want a written report from *you* on all this."

"Okay."

"How'd you find out all this stuff?" Harry asked. "Brainwash the guy? All you Chinese go in for that, they tell me."

Ah Lee laughed. "I showed up a little early last night at my rendezvous with Soon Fat and Bailey. Hung around a back alley till I saw Bailey go into Soon Fat's through the back door. Followed him in and eavesdropped through the door of the room where I was told to meet them. Nothing to it, Harry. But I sure want you to lay it on those people good."

Harry yelled, "I intend to, Lee, I intend to! Can't touch Kai San . . . was that his name? . . . or Soon Fat in Montreal, of course."

"Give Ottawa the Soon Fat information, Harry. Maybe they will reason with him."

"That's a thought. On the other hand, I can come down on this Roger Bailey myself, him being an American citizen and all."

"Come down on him hard," Ah Lee said. "Hard, Harry."

"Some special reason?"

"You could say so. Murder one. Or manslaughter at the least, on top of the smuggling rap. Remember the two Chinese boys you found frozen to death near North Troy last winter?"

"I remember."

"Bailey sent them across, but he didn't bother to pick them up on this side. Just let them freeze to death."

"Well, well." Harry's great voice all at once held a thread of iron. "You find out why?"

"He knew beforehand you were going to be patrolling the North Troy area that night, Harry. So after he sent the boys walking across the line, he just went home to bed. The hell with the Chinese aliens."

"Now, now, Lee, don't be bitter. You want me to

think you're a racist?" Harry was silent for a moment. At length he boomed, "I must say you earned your pay, Lee."

"I'm sorry about one thing, though."

"What's that?"

"There's got to be a leak in your office somewhere, Harry, don't you see?"

"I see," Harry said with a snort. "You think I'm a moron? This Bailey knew ahead of time about our border patrol at North Troy last winter when your Chinese froze. He knew ahead of time nobody would bother you last night at Derby Line. You let me worry about that, Lee. I kind of got it solved already, matter of fact."

Ah Lee was surprised. "You have?"

"Sure," Harry shouted into the phone. "You know that blonde filing clerk we got in Records?

"No."

"Well, her name happens to be Mrs. Roger Bailey, Lee. How does that grab you?"

"I wish I had your brains," Ah Lee said, laughing. "Then I could sit in a comfortable office solving mysteries instead of working my rear off on a Chinese freighter."

"That won't hurt you. You always were a little squirt, Lee. The exercise probably did you a lot of good."

Ah Lee grinned. "Maybe. But I didn't tell you the good part, Harry."

"There was a good part?"

"I lived in a Chinese bordello in Montreal for five days."

Harry roared with laughter. "Ain't you ashamed of yourself? A bordello! That's a hell of a way for a deputy regional commissioner of the U.S. Immigration and Naturalization Service to carry on!"

"I'm sorry, Mr. Commissioner," Ah Lee said sharply. "I won't let it happen again."

SWAMP RAT

by C. B. Gilford

In the dark, dripping night the yelping of the blood-hounds was the only sound. Far off? Harmless? Going in another direction? He couldn't tell. He couldn't tell anything. He wasn't even sure by this time whether he was headed in the right direction.

Get a grip, Claude boy, he told himself. Run scared, yes, but don't get confused. Maybe they'll get you, but don't make it easy for them. Don't walk right into their arms.

Remember, Claude boy, like the old-timers always said, if you could make it as far as the swamp, you were halfway to freedom—and you're here, Claude boy, you're in the swamp. Those dogs may sound fearful, but they can't follow a scent through water. Oh sure, the guards will go around, will try to be there when you come out on dry ground. The dogs will try to pick up the trail again. But there are a thousand places where you might hit the dry ground again. The odds are on your side, boy.

Yet the sound of the dogs was getting closer! It was! There were spots of dry ground—paths—all through the swamp. The dogs had lost the scent, but they were running over those paths now, trying to find it again. He'd crossed some of those paths, then plunged into stagnant pools again. They might find his trail.

Flashlights . . . any sign of flashlights? No, nothing. The blackness was complete. He'd chosen this night because it was so dark, no moon, no stars. So dark that now and then he stumbled into logs, stumps, overhanging branches that lashed at his face, grabbed his clothes. He forged ahead, trying more than anything else to travel in a straight line.

Then he sensed it. Something . . . a presence . . . just off to his left . . . a shadow darker than the rest of the darkness. He halted, and the little gurgling sounds his legs made going through the knee-deep water stopped. For a moment the dogs had ceased barking, so the whole swamp was deathly still.

The presence was silent too, but Claude knew it was there. A tall column of black . . . not a tree, though just as motionless. Claude waited, not breathing. If it was a live thing, a man, it would have to move, reveal itself. So he had to wait, to outwait the thing.

Then the dogs started again, closer still! They'd surely found his trail, for they were coming straight in his direction, while he was being held at bay, unable to move . . .

"You breakin' out, mister?"

The sudden question came in scarcely more than a whisper, but it startled him as completely as if it had been a gunshot. He stood transfixed, wanting to run first, then not wanting to, afraid that the man, whoever it was, would have a gun. But he wasn't a guard, for the guards had dogs. What kind of eyesight did he have, though, to find somebody in this darkness? How could Claude ever escape from eyesight like that?

"I asked you a question, mister. Are you breakin' out?"

Still he couldn't answer.

"Well, you got to be, I reckon. The dogs are yippin', and here you are, wadin' through the swamp. Nobody ever wanders through here at night unless he's breakin' out of the place. What's your name?"

There was a kind of authority in the voice now that compelled answers. "Claude Wetzel." He whispered too.

"Crime?"

"Armed robbery."

"How long are you in for?"

"Fifteen."

"And if they catch you, there won't be time off for good behavior. Right?"

There was a soft chuckle in the voice. It was the voice of an older man. How old? Old enough to run away from? No . . . he could have a gun . . . and for certain he had eyes that could see in the dark. But there was a possible friendliness in the voice. Why friendly? No reason. Still, this guy wasn't yelling for the guards. So Claude had to go on answering the questions. There wasn't much choice.

"How old are you?"

"Nineteen."

A silence, punctuated by yelping from the dogs, ever closer. Then the comment, "Got in trouble early, didn't you?"

Was there a touch of sadness in the voice now? Sympathy? Maybe this old guy wouldn't call the guards, would let an escapee go past him. Maybe he'd even point the quickest direction out of the swamp!

"Too young for that place!" Claude burst out. "I couldn't stand it. I made a mistake, sure, but you can bet I won't make another one so they can send me back there."

Again the soft chuckle. "Except what you're tryin' to do right now, huh?"

Claude took the gamble. "They're gettin' pretty close," he said. "Are you goin' to call 'em and tell 'em where I am?"

Now it was the other's turn not to answer. There was silence between them for a moment. Claude tried to be patient, but with those dogs not far away, it wasn't easy. Then without warning, a light blazed in his eyes. Only a flashlight, but it blinded him. He cursed, tried to turn away from it, but the beam stayed on him for maybe ten seconds before it clicked out.

"They saw that for sure," he complained angrily, starting to splash through the water again.

The other's voice stopped him. "They didn't see it. There's a big tangle of trees between them and us. Slow down, sonny. I know what I'm doin'. They didn't see it, I tell you. I just wanted to get a look at you."

"Okay, you got your look. I'm goin'."

"Slow down, I said." The voice was authoritative again. "I wanted to look at you, and now I did. So you don't have to go."

Claude backed up a step. He was suspicious, wary, alert for danger. "What do you mean?"

"I'm goin' to help you. Give you a place to hide."

"No thanks. I've got to get movin'."

"Too late, sonny. You ain't been movin' fast enough up to now. They'll cut you off for sure. While you're splashin' around, they're runnin' over the dry paths."

"I've got to take a chance."

"Okay." The voice was sad. "It's your funeral."

Claude didn't go. The guy had sounded sincere. Maybe he was right. There were dry paths through the swamp, and the guards would know them. They could travel faster than he could. Maybe they could cut him off. He hadn't gotten the head start he had hoped to. Maybe he did need help.

"Why should you help me?" he demanded.

" 'Cause I don't like that place. I know what them places are like. Five years I had. And I don't like them guards. I've seen what they do. And I don't like them dogs. Them I like least of all."

"But why me? Why help me?"

" 'Cause you're a youngster. Maybe if you got free you'd go straight. If you went back they'd ruin you for sure. 'Sides, I like your looks. That's why I turned the light on you. Wanted to see what you looked like. You look okay. Maybe you're worth helpin'."

It sounded crazy, plain crazy. "Wouldn't you get in trouble yourself?" Claude wanted to know.

"I know what I'm doin'," the other said. "I know

how them guards work. And I know this swamp even better than they do. I live here. Come on, boy, we're wastin' time. Take it or leave it."

Claude Wetzel thought for a minute. The dogs sounded now as if they weren't more than a hundred yards away. He speedily took it.

His new friend had specific plans and instructions. Claude wasn't to walk any farther. He wasn't to leave any more trail for the dogs. Instead he was to be carried.

His benefactor sloshed into the water and lifted him easily, slung him like a sack of grain over his shoulder. He was obviously a strong man, and Claude couldn't help wondering whether he'd made a mistake accepting this man's help. He was totally in his physical power now, maybe headed back toward the prison walls.

They were going somewhere at a good rate. Even in the dark the older man seemed to know all the paths. Never once did they blunder into water or slime. They went silently, with the dogs baying off to the right, close, but not any closer than before.

Claude knew that they had arrived at their destination only when the man hesitated, stopped when his feet came into contact with a hard surface, probably wood, then ascended several steps. A door swung shut behind them. Claude was lowered gently to a standing position on the floor.

His host took a step or two away. A match was struck. In the sudden glare Claude was blinded. He could only follow the flame as it traveled a few inches, then applied itself to the wick of a kerosene lamp. The flame grew, whitened, till it illuminated the area around it.

He saw the man then. Certainly no superman, he was actually a small fellow, an inch or two shorter than Claude. Dressed in an old slouch hat, ragged, rumpled shirt and trousers, he had a wrinkled little face, framed in a half-moon of gray beard stubble.

Maybe the guy was fifty, maybe seventy.

The room wasn't any fancier than the man, with plank walls and floor, furniture mostly different size boxes, a larger one for the table where the lamp sat, a couple of smaller ones for seats, a cot over to one side, with a dirty blanket on it, a lot of junk around . . . an old stove, bottles, cans . . . just junk.

"Welcome to my house, Claude," the man was saying. "We're sort of on the edge of the swamp if you want to know where we are. Now, I'm goin' to leave the light on. They'll be comin' by. They'd stop here anyway, but they'll be a lot less likely to want to come inside if the light's on and things look normal. Sometimes you got to be bold. That confuses 'em. But don't you worry, I'll take care of 'em. Now just crawl under that cot. Let the blanket hang over the side and they won't see you if they look through the door."

"Hide under the cot!" Claude exploded. "That's too simple!"

"It's bein' bold," the old man argued. "Now if you want to change your mind, boy, I'll show you which way to go, and you can make a run for it."

At that moment there was a sudden angry yelping of dogs that sounded like it was right outside. Claude dived under the cot, frantically reached for the filthy blanket and pulled it down between himself and the light of the kerosene lamp. He lay there shaking, trembling with the combined cold of terror and the wet of the swamp.

By the time he had arranged his concealment, the clamor of the dogs surrounded the shack. They can smell me, Claude thought wildly, and wanted to shriek out his surrender and plead for mercy. They can smell me right through the cracks in these boards. That stupid old idiot, bringing me here . . . it's a trap . . . nobody could be that stupid . . . yes, they could . . . he himself was that stupid . . . thinking he could hide instead of running . . . damn that old man . . .

He couldn't see anything. The blanket hid the world from him just as it hid him from the world. He could only hear. The dogs seemed to have approached from the rear of the shack, then poured around both sides toward the front.

Other sounds, the shouts and curses of men, the guards who held the leashes and now seemed to be trying to quiet the dogs. . . .

Where was the old man? What was he doing? Signaling the guards, trying to tell them over all the noise that the escaped con was inside the shack? Pointing to the cot under which he was hiding?

"Hey, Dad!"

It was shouted several times, and then finally the frenzied baying and yelping lessened, though the bloodhounds kept whimpering and growling. Now human voices could make themselves heard.

"Hey, Dad!"

"What're you boys doin' out at this time of night? Givin' them dogs some exercise?"

"Man went over the wall, Dad."

"You don't say. Here I was thinkin' these critters was makin' all this fuss over me. Look out there, Sam, you keep that Black Susan away from me now. She'll tear off these pants of mine, and I ain't got no other pair. Keep a good hold on her, Sam . . . old bitch never did like me . . ."

A laugh came from the guard. "That's 'cause you stink up this swamp so much, Dad. You put so much stink in the air that when old Susan here has a job to do, she has a hard time smellin' anything else. You take a bath once in a while, Dad, and she'll like you better. Maybe it would do no good though. They say an old con never loses his prison stink."

There was a pause in the human conversation, and savage snarling from a dog.

"You ain't seen nobody, have you, Dad?" the guard queried.

"Not a soul. How many's gone?"

"Just one this time."

"Well, I ain't seen even one."

"Sure of that?"

"Course I'm sure. Wish you boys would keep better locks on your doors. I don't like to be waked up in the middle of the night with all the commotion them damn dogs of yours make."

The dog chorus rose in volume again then. The guards yelled at the dogs, seemed to be pulling them away, for slowly—too slowly for Claude Wetzel—the whole bedlam receded.

For a long time afterward, however, there were scattered sounds, quick yelps from the dogs, an occasional shout from the guards. The search party was trying to pick up the trail again. Finally the door swung closed, and the sounds dwindled still further.

"Reckon you can come out of there, Claude."

Claude pushed the blanket a little aside, and blinked in the soft glow cast by the kerosene lamp. Still cautiously, still hardly believing that for the moment at least he was safe, he crawled out from under the cot.

"Them dogs'll be roamin' the swamp the rest of the night," the old man said, taking a seat on one of the boxes, "but it ain't likely they'll be comin' back this way. You could get yourself some sleep, Claude. I'll set and watch out for 'em."

Claude stood up. He was trying to sort out everything in his mind. "Them guards know you were a con, huh?" he asked finally.

The old fellow grinned. The grin showed his teeth, or what was left of them. "Sure they do," he said. "That's what fools 'em, you see. I knew it would. Maybe those dogs could smell you in here. I'll bet old Black Susan could. That's one of the reasons she got so excited. But they thought she was just smellin' me."

Claude stared at his host in wonderment. "Does a man who's been in prison really have a convict smell the rest of his life? Is that why that dog don't like you?"

The broken-toothed grin widened half an inch. "Dogs are smarter'n most humans," the old fellow answered. "I don't think I got no prison stink on me no more. Even if I did, the swamp stink would have covered it up by now. It's been a long time since I've been in."

"Why don't that dog like you then?" Claude persisted.

The old man hesitated. Maybe now he was being careful. "Dogs are smart, like I said," he replied finally, "and that Black Susan is smarter'n most dogs. Maybe she knows I'm an enemy. I'm helpin' you, ain't I? I ain't on her side. Dogs know things like that."

Now that he seemed safe, at least temporarily, Claude's brain began to function. A suspicion, maybe an explanation, had sneaked into his mind. "You ever been an enemy of that dog before?" he asked. "You ever helped anybody on a breakout before?"

The old man didn't say anything, but his eyes had narrowed.

"What do you get out of it?" Claude went on. He was young, but he had lived long enough to realize that nobody took such risks for nothing. "What do I got to pay you, Dad? Dad, that's what they call you, ain't it? What's the price, Dad?"

The old man turned away. "Get some sleep, boy. You're goin' to need your legs in the mornin'."

But next morning Claude Wetzel didn't leave the shack. The bloodhounds were still baying, and they weren't very far away.

"I guess they think you never made it to the road," Dad said. "They think you're still in the swamp, I reckon."

Claude didn't like the idea of staying. As long as he remained here he belonged to the old man. So far so good, but he didn't know what the old fellow might have in mind or how he might trick him.

Funny guy. He'd heard on the inside that there was an old man who lived in a shack sort of on the edge of the swamp, but nobody had ever suggested that he might help an escaping prisoner. Seemed like if he was a friend of the cons the word might have gotten around.

Claude decided not to ask any more questions that day. No use in asking questions anyway if they weren't answered. Instead, he accepted breakfast. The old fellow cooked on the stove, a wood-burner, and the place filled with smoke, but the meat and the beans, both out of cans, were filling. There was a cardboard box full of canned food, he noticed.

After breakfast the day passed slowly. Every once in a while the bloodhounds bayed, sometimes far off, sometimes nearer. Claude listened, and decided to stay put.

"They can still smell you," Dad explained. "They're picking up pieces of your trail where you crossed dry ground. Sounds like maybe you didn't always go in a straight line."

"How long can them dogs keep on smellin' me?" Claude wanted to know.

Old Dad shrugged. "Who knows about dogs?"

"How long'll them guards keep on lookin'?"

"Who knows about them either? They don't like people breakin' out of their place. Them guards and them hounds are kind of alike. Hurts their pride, I reckon, when somebody makes a good break."

Claude stayed on through the rest of the day. Once he emerged from the swamp, he knew, it would be more than five miles to the road. He had no clothes except his prison clothes, no money. It might take him a while to find clothes and then a ride. The dogs, still wandering around, would be on his trail. He had to stay.

The old man didn't seem to mind sharing his food. In fact, he seemed willing to trade the food, as well as the risk, for the company of another human being.

They didn't talk much, but old Dad seemed to enjoy waiting on his guest, fixing and serving his food, bringing him water, just watching him.

"What if they come back and find me here?" Claude asked once. "What'll they do to you?"

"Nothin' prob'ly."

"What do you mean?"

"I'll tell 'em you dropped in just a few minutes before they came. I'll tell 'em I would have called them except that you threatened me with a knife."

"But I don't have a knife."

The old man took a long butcher knife out of one of the many cardboard cartons, tossed it on the box where they ate. "I'll tell 'em you grabbed that one," he said.

Claude Wetzel stared at the knife for a long time. He'd keep track of where that knife stayed at all times, he decided. It might come in handy in different ways than the way old Dad had mentioned.

The guards and the dogs returned finally, three days later. They arrived at dawn, just as the first rays of the sun started filtering through the thick swamp foliage. They must have approached silently, for neither Claude nor the old man heard them. They might have gotten all the way inside without being heard if the dogs—or at least one dog, Black Susan—hadn't begun to growl ferociously just outside the door.

Claude was lying on the cot. Dad had insisted that he sleep on the cot while he himself curled up on some papers and rags on the hard floor. At Black Susan's throaty snarl, Claude instinctively rolled off the bunk, then beneath, arranging the blanket to conceal himself as before. Dad, meanwhile, had leaped up and was at the door before any guard could barge in.

"Now don't go and tell me, Sam," Claude could hear the old man dodging with his guests, "that you've gone and misplaced another prisoner. Gettin' mighty careless."

The noises Black Susan was making were un-

friendly. "Nope," Sam answered, "we're still lookin'
around for Claude Wetzel."

"Same one?"

"Same one. Ain't had no reports of him from anywhere around. No cars stolen. No clothes stolen. No
money stolen. None of the farmers have seen him. So
he's got to be hidin' in the swamp."

A chill ran through Claude. Too late! He should
have known better! He should have taken off in the
middle of the night one night, and walked, just
walked, taken no money, clothes, or cars, just walked
. . . for a hundred miles.

"Been three or four days, ain't it?" Dad was asking
easily, calmly, joking with them.

"That's right," the guard said. "He ought to be
pretty hungry by now. I was wondering if he maybe
stopped by your place for a bite to eat."

Black Susan, as if she sensed the accusing tone in the
guard's voice, growled menacingly.

"This ain't no restaurant," Dad assured the guard.
"Now, Sam, you keep that dog off me, you hear?"

The guard laughed. "Dad," he said, "if I'd ever
catch you helpin' a con, I'd let these dogs at you. You
hear me?"

"I hear you, Sam."

The party left then. Black Susan departed with re-
luctance. Her disappointment was audible for five
minutes as her leash pulled her back toward home.

When the swamp was silent again, Dad came inside.
He was wearing his satisfied grin.

"They're sure mad," he said. "They keep on lookin'
and sayin' you're still in the swamp, but that's because
they don't like to admit that you got away."

"But I ain't got away," Claude argued. He felt relief
for the moment, but he still had plenty of problems.
"I got a long way to go yet. I got no money, clothes,
nothin'."

"Ain't no hurry, is there, Claude?" Old Dad sat

down on a box, acting kind of shy. "You can stay here as long as you like . . ."

"Look, Dad," Claude said angrily, "I didn't break out of that place so I could spend the rest of my life in a swamp. This is almost as bad as inside."

The old man looked hurt. "But like you said, you got no money or anythin'."

"I'll find what I need."

"Well, maybe I can help you there too."

"Huh?"

"Maybe, if you give me a little time, I could scout around. Find you some clothes for sure." Dad hesitated, rubbed the gray stubble on his chin. "Might scare up a little piece of change somewhere too . . ."

"Where?" Claude was excited now.

"Now never mind. Fact is, though, Claude, you need me. I can fix you up when the time comes. 'Sides that, you need me to show you the way out of here. Maybe you don't know it, and maybe you never heard anybody say it, but they run those dogs more times than just when there's a breakout. Dogs need exercise, for one thing. And they kind of patrol too—every night—just in case somebody's slipped away they don't know about. 'Sides that, they're still lookin' for you."

Once again Claude had no choice. He had to wait. The old man was right, he knew. The dogs might be out anytime. He'd wait till his trail cooled.

But now he had another reason for staying. What had Dad said? "Might scare you up a little piece of change . . ." Now where did Dad get all those canned goods they were eating? Didn't seem he had any job, no way to make a living. Then he had to have money, maybe a lot of money. A crazy old hermit who liked to live all alone in the swamp here . . . He'd been inside once, hadn't he? Maybe he was still living off the swag from the job that had put him inside in the first place. Crazier things happen, don't they?

It took Claude nearly two weeks to decide for sure

there was only one place from which the old man could scare up money. The bankroll had to be there in the shack.

In that two weeks Dad made two trips away from the shack. Each time he took a gunnysack with him. He always went at a time when he was pretty sure, he said, that the guards and the dogs wouldn't be nosing around. He promised not to be gone long.

Those were two times, of course, that Claude had had an opportunity to make his break, but he didn't have the money and clothes he needed. Without them his chances weren't good, but if he got them, his chances would be a lot better. So he waited.

Dad never stayed away long; a couple of hours each time. On both occasions the dogs remained silent and the swamp empty. Dad could have run to that guard Sam. But Claude didn't think he would do that, and he didn't.

Dad brought back food, stuff in cans mostly. He explained that there was a small general store down on the road. Claude was sure then. Storekeepers don't give credit to old guys like Dad, and Dad obviously didn't work for the things he brought home. So he had paid in hard cash. Money.

On the second trip, at Claude's insistence, Dad came back with a work shirt and a pair of work trousers. He'd had to get his own sizes, he said, to avoid suspicion. Claude was a little taller than the old man, but the fit was close enough. Slipping out of the prison denims and into this new khaki outfit, he felt he was ready to travel. All he needed now was a little spending money.

He knew now the only place it could possibly be. He'd used Dad's two absences to look for it here, but no use. The old man carried it on him.

He managed to wait till after supper though. They'd feasted on sausage, canned tomatoes, canned peaches, and a loaf of fresh bread. The old man had used the butcher knife to sever the sausage links.

Claude took possession of the knife, and when Dad looked up from the last of his peaches, he saw the knife pointing at him.

"I'm leaving tonight, Dad," Claude said. "I need money."

The old man looked pained. He leaned back against the board wall. "I told you I was goin' to help you."

"I want the help now."

"Didn't I bring you them clothes?"

"I need money, too. I know you got it around here someplace."

"How you goin' to get by the dogs, boy?"

"They make plenty of noise. I'll stay clear of 'em."

"Think you can do that?"

"Don't change the subject, Dad. I want the money."

The old man gazed down at the empty can of peaches. "I guess I knew you'd do it this way sooner or later," he said, almost to himself. Then he looked up suddenly, determination substituting for the pain in his face. "Can't let you do it, Claude. You got to wait till mornin' at least. Dogs are out tonight."

Yeah, sure the dogs were out. And the old man would yell for them sure enough if Claude headed out the door to freedom, because he didn't want Claude to leave. He liked company here in this shack. So he'd yell, unless he couldn't . . .

Claude reached across the box that was their supper table, and pushed the point of the knife between the old man's ribs. The movement was so swift that all Dad could do was to follow the path of the blade with his eyes. Then he stared down at the handle clasped in Claude's fist, and finally saw the steel withdrawn, carrying the stain of his life's blood with it.

"Claude . . ."

Dad didn't fall. He was wedged into a corner and remained upright. Claude dropped the knife on the table-box and began feeling Dad's pockets. It was half a minute before he noticed that Dad was still alive, eyes open, and shaking his head.

The voice that came out of the grizzled beard-stubble was barely audible. "Nothin' here, Claude," the voice said. "Joe Crawford . . . storekeeper . . . he's postmaster too . . . he's got a safe . . . everything's there . . ."

Claude drew back and gazed at the old man in horror. How was he going to get anywhere without money? He'd have to get it from that storekeeper . . . or somebody . . . but it wouldn't be easy. Those things are always more successful when there's a chance to plan.

He wanted to stab the old man again, to punish him, make him pay. "If you'd really wanted to help me," he screamed, "you'd have brought me the money like I asked you!"

He would have stabbed him again, but the faraway baying of bloodhounds interrupted. He stood still, nerves twanging.

"Hear 'em?" the old man whispered.

Yes, he heard them. But far away . . . he could avoid them . . .

"Tell you somethin'," the old man was saying softly. "Guess it don't matter now. It's important to you, boy. I broke out myself . . ."

Claude looked at the old man again.

"Broke out of this same place . . . nearly nine years ago now . . ." The effort to speak had brought a trickle of blood to the corner of his mouth. It foamed out slowly, staining his gray stubble. "Broke out . . . and they never caught me . . ."

The old man was lying, but it didn't concern Claude anyway. He wanted to listen for the dogs, but he found himself listening to Dad too. "Sure," he jeered, "and you came back to live right next door to the place."

The old man nodded. "I did it," he gasped out painfully, " 'cause I had my kid brother inside . . . I was goin' to help him when he made his break . . . he never made it though . . . died inside there so I stayed here . . ."

Something had clicked in Claude's brain. "That guard Sam knows you were a con. How come he doesn't bother you, lets you stay here?"

A bubble of blood burst on the old man's lips. Behind it his words came weaker than before, almost inaudible. "Sam knows I was a con . . . had to tell him somethin' . . . 'cause of the way Black Susan was actin' . . . Sam didn't remember chasin' me . . . but Black Susan did . . . she was mad . . . still is . . . you saw her . . . so I told Sam she could still smell the prison stink on me . . . Sam thought that was funny . . . but I know better . . . that old bitch never forgets the smell of an escaped man . . ."

Claude backed away, but the failing voice pursued him, like the whisper of death.

"Old Susan tracked me to the store once . . . still rememberin' . . . I knew what she was doin' . . . Sam never did catch on . . . When you left, boy, I was goin' to make a false trail . . . lead Susan away from your trail . . . can't do it now, though . . . don't let her get a sniff of you tonight, boy, or . . . she'll come after you . . ."

He was out of the swamp now. He'd made it, and he still had his directions straight. Five miles to the road, then he'd walk. He had no money, so he had to walk, because he didn't dare leave a trail of robbery and more violence behind him. He'd walk a hundred miles. He started out on the first mile.

Then he heard it: a sudden eerie canine cry of discovery, exultation, triumph. He had been expecting it, really, but he began running anyway, and he kept on, even as the sound came closer.